Annie Thomas

Allerton Towers

A Novel: Vol. I.

Annie Thomas

Allerton Towers
A Novel: Vol. I.

ISBN/EAN: 9783337054595

Printed in Europe, USA, Canada, Australia, Japan

Cover: Foto ©Andreas Hilbeck / pixelio.de

More available books at **www.hansebooks.com**

ALLERTON TOWERS.

A Novel.

By ANNIE THOMAS

(Mrs. Pender Cudlip),

AUTHOR OF "DENIS DONNE," "PLAYED OUT," "EYRE OF BLENDON," ETC.

IN THREE VOLUMES.

VOL. I.

LONDON:

TINSLEY BROTHERS, 8, CATHERINE STREET, STRAND.

1882.

CONTENTS.

ALLERTON TOWERS.

CHAPTER I.

"WALTER, I may as well tell you that mother thinks we have been very premature and foolish."

"And I may as well tell you, Ethel, that your mother shows great want of consistency in saying so."

"Mother doesn't go in for being consistent," the girl laughs, joyously; "she speaks and acts on impulse as a rule, and this morning she told me she had one of her strong intuitions against our being engaged; you see your practice isn't much yet, Walter; mother's only prudent after all."

"And do you want to be prudent too, Ethel?" he asks, and his voice trembles a little as he manfully strives to steady it.

His feelings are being cruelly assailed by the remarks which the girl to whom he has been engaged a week is repeating so carelessly.

She laughs again, but her mirth is not quite spontaneous.

"I don't want to plunge into poverty, I must admit."

"Poverty! a day or two ago you were willing enough to face the future with me, darling; what has changed you? Your mother was satisfied with the prospect I offered then; what has made her dissatisfied with it now? I can give you a good home, surround you with every comfort." He pauses abruptly, for Ethel's eyes and attention are evidently wandering back to a group on the lawn, the centre of which is a young, handsome man of unmistakably "good form," to whose utterances all the girls who grace Mrs. Heatherley's garden party are listening with almost too flattering attention.

"Who's that fellow?" Walter Gifford— the young surgeon, who has within the last six months made himself a medical power in this district—asks pugnaciously, and Ethel Heatherley answers, in a state of tremulous excitement,

"Don't you know? that is Lord Marcus Boyne—the Marquis of Monkstown's second son."

"Now I know why your mother has grown prudent so suddenly," Mr. Gifford says, quietly. Then he takes Ethel's small hands in his, and holds her fast while he says. "Why has Mrs. Heatherley got that good-looking boy here to dazzle all you girls? he's a young scamp, Ethel, sent here to do penance at poor old Townley's, for having been a naughty boy at Oxford; he has a courtesy title and eighty pounds a-year, and your mother wants you to throw me over for him!"

"You're very rude, Walter," Ethel says, her cheeks growing crimson in a condemnatory way at once; "mother has asked him here as she always asks Mr. Townley's pupils; she can't help his being attentive and handsome and having a title, and—and how do you dare to imply that dear mother is a match-maker?"

" Don't get savage, Ethel——"

" Then don't you be jealous ! "

As the girl says this, there flutters towards them one of the prettiest and youngest-looking of matrons. Mrs. Heatherley, who has a well-grown daughter of twenty, looks at the first glance little more than thirty herself, for she has the fair beauty and the slenderness of limb which makes middle-age pass for youth.

Dressed to perfection to-day in pink sateen with pockets and cuffs and piping of ruby velvet, the pretty blonde widow commands almost as much admiration as does her beautiful brunette daughter Ethel, as she flits hither and thither on her closely-shaven lawn, seeing to the amusement and well-being of her guests.

She has achieved a great social success. The lord-lieutenant of the county and his wife are here, and the Bishop of Allerton Towers and his daughter; and, indeed, everybody who is anybody in all the region round has accepted her invitation for lawn-tennis and strawberries and cream this day. But she feels a crumple in her rose-leaf! Her only child has just before wilfully engaged herself to a hard-working young country surgeon, and now a marquis's son has come and found her fair.

Such a marquis's son too! It is all very well for malignant envy and jealousy to sneer, and hint that the Marquis of Monkstown derives his income from Irish property—the rents of which are not paid in these days.

Mrs. Heatherley knows better. His lordship is no mere feckless, improvident, out-at-elbows Irish peer! Mrs. Heatherley has it on Mrs. Townley's authority that he has to do, surreptitiously, but remuneratively, with indigo and coffee, and that he can snap his fingers at his non-rent-paying tenants. The eldest son, Lord E. Kenmare, is delicate, if not imbecile, and Lord Marcus is the second son—and—well—

"A coronet would become Ethel well, and it's not with my consent that she shall throw herself away on a mere country practitioner," the ambitious lady tells herself; and immediately afterwards she makes that remark to

Ethel, as to their having been very premature and foolish in engaging themselves to one another, which Ethel has frankly repeated to her lover.

As Mrs. Heatherley flutters up to the young pair, into the music of whose love and contentment she has introduced a discordant strain, she looks so gladly and gaily unconscious of having said or done anything antagonistic to Mr. Gifford's interests, that he is almost inclined to believe that she is as well pleased with the engagement as she professed herself to be at first. Such a dear little airy impulsive woman! So evidently quick to feel, and prompt to act as her feelings dictate! Her future son-in-law can but admire her, and think that his Ethel has perverted her mother's meaning, rather than think Mrs. Heatherley is either inconsistent, or foolish enough to wish to displace him for Lord Marcus Boyne.

Her first words make him change this view of things.

"My dear Mr. Gifford," she begins, in her bright, electrical, young way, "*do* forgive me

for putting your interest before your pleasure;
I am going to take you away from Ethel, and
introduce you to the Bishop and Miss Templeton : he is a martyr to the gout, you
know, the dear old thing, and if you are
called in at the Palace, the whole of Allerton Towers will be sending for you ; Ethel,
Miss Templeton has been sitting alone for the
last ten minutes ! I can't be everywhere,
can I?" she continues, appealingly; " so
you must sacrifice yourself a little to our
guests."

" The Bishop hasn't the gout at the present
moment, so he dosen't want me, and Miss
Templeton is exercising her maidenly wiles
on Townley's new cub, so she doesn't want
Ethel," Walter Gifford says, in a way that
implies, under these circumstances, he means
to keep Ethel to himself—apart from the
others—a little longer.

Mrs. Heatherley makes a face expressive
of excruciating suffering, and then explains
the cause of it.

" It would give me *intense* pain if the
St. Justs and the Bishop remark that my

daughter neglects her social duties," she says, seriously ; " and as Ethel would not wish me to feel pain or annoyance on her account, she will do as I wish her, of course ; and you really *must* let me introduce you to his lordship."

She puts a coaxing hand on the young man's arm as she speaks, and he feels himself being slowly but surely propelled towards the ecclesiastical potentate whose patronage she professes to be anxious to secure for him. Meantime, he sees Ethel going off in the direction of Miss Templeton, who is bending a gracious ear to all the folly it pleases Lord Marcus to utter. Walter Gifford's prophetically-jealous heart whispers to him, that not for many minutes longer will the Bishop's daughter have the opportunity of so visibly condescending to a mere man. For Ethel has the winning power to a rare degree, and Walter knows, from sweetly bitter experience, that it is not in her gracious nature to refrain from exercising it.

He is introduced to the Bishop, who is urbane to, but evidently uninterested in, him ;

in spite of the eulogistic words which Mrs. Heatherley speaks of him.

"My lord, allow me to introduce a friend of mine, Mr. Gifford, one of the few people who makes this wilderness of Allerton endurable and pleasant to me."

In response to this direct call upon his proverbial urbanity, the Bishop smiles briefly, says "he is happy, he is sure, to make the acquaintance of anyone who is fortunate enough to find favour in Mrs. Heatherley's eyes;" and then, having been previously apprised as to the calling of the young man, who is now supposed to be a suppliant for his favour, goes on to say that he hopes "he finds the climate salubrious and the population healthy."

"The instinct of self-preservation makes me regret that I am able to answer your lordship's hopes satisfactorily," Walter says, savagely; for Ethel, Miss Templeton, and Lord Marcus Boyne have just sauntered up to the group of which he is one, and he sees a look of merrily-malicious amusement in Ethel's brown velvet eyes, at the way in which her mother is striving to make him perform for patronage.

"It's just like papa always to say the wrong thing to people of that sort," Miss Templeton mutters to Lord Marcus, and Ethel hears the words and understands their full meaning.

Her colour rises with her generous wrath. Shall she stand by and hear the position of her lover—the man to whom her troth is plighted!—assailed, without saying one word of rebuke? or shall she spare the assailant, who is her guest, according to the dictates of hospitality? For a moment she wavers, then she says:

"What sort of people does the Bishop say the right thing to, Miss Templeton?"

"Oh, to our own class, or the *very* poor, papa is always happy in his expressions, and just what he should be in manner; but to people of that sort" (and Miss Templeton, as she speaks, nods her head towards the young surgeon) "the Bishop is apt to be uncomfortable."

"Local apothecary, isn't he?" Lord Marcus asks, tersely.

" Yes," Ethel says, facing him in her perfect prettiness and irreproachable style, " that, if you please to call him so; and something else, as I please to call him; the man who is going to marry me, by-and-bye!—my 'sweetheart,' in our plain old country vulgar tongue."

The young fellow she addresses is very handsome, very thoroughbred, very fascinating and dazzling in his gay, bright way, but he is very boyish still! Consequently, he bursts into a loud, rather derisive laugh, and says:

"Come, now, Miss Heatherley, don't chaff a fellow too much; *you* going to marry a 'local practitioner,' that's too awfully awful a joke."

" But I *am*," Ethel is saying, with steady severity, when her mother again intervenes.

Flitting up in the most guileless way possible, the active little parent-bird is by the side of the brave but injudicious young one in a moment.

"Ethel, dear, Lady St. Just was saying just now, she had not spoken a word to you to-

day; go to her, my child: Miss Templeton
and Lord Marcus" (this with ever so sweet a
smile) " will excuse you, I am sure.   Lady St.
Just is quite another mother to my child," the
vivacious little hostess says, fluttering in between her two guests, and contriving to direct
Lord Marcus's attention to the graceful way
in which Ethel is crossing the lawn towards
martial-looking Lady St. Just.

" Then she's prepared to adopt 'Sawbones,'
too, I suppose ? " Lord Marcus says, impru-
dently.   He has yet to learn that Mrs.
Heatherley can snub as well as she can
court.

" What a nice, unsophisticated boy you
are," she says, innocently ignoring the fact
that youth objects to few things so much as
having itself forced crudely into the fierce
light of sarcastic observation; "it's an old
joke from *Pickwick* to call a surgeon a 'sawbones,'" she continues, in an explanatory
tone, to Miss Templeton ; isn't it refreshing
to meet with any young man in these days
who is sufficiently world-worn to quote such
nearly-forgotten witticisms? "

Her tone is so full of feminine kindness as she speaks her biting words, that Lord Marcus is undecided whether he ought to hate her for the rudeness, which *may* be unintentional, and which is making him smart, or like her for the liking she expresses so openly for him! Eventually he decides in favour of doing the latter, for, besides having the claim to manly toleration of being a pretty woman still, she is Ethel's mother! And already his heart has gone out to Ethel, with a young man's pure, adoring, but still passionate love.

So, with the courtesy of his caste, he accepts the snub so gracefully and graciously, that Mrs. Heatherley is half inclined to regret having given it to him.

"If you had called me 'vulgarly malicious,' instead of 'nice and unsophisticated,' you would have been nearer the mark, Mrs. Heatherley," he says, with proud boyish candour. "I won't err again in your estimation —at least, not in that way."

"And on my side I promise to look very leniently on your errors," Mrs. Heatherley says,

softly, but not so softly but that Miss Templeton hears the words, and malignantly repeats
them, by-and-bye, to her right-reverend father,
whom she undutifully suspects of a desire to
change his state, whenever he sees much of
the late Mr. Heatherley's agreeable and good-
looking little relict.

Meantime, the onus of sustaining a conversation with a man who evidently labours
strenuously to converse with him, is becoming
a burden, heavier than he can bear, to Walter
Gifford. With that fatal perspicuity, which
is one of the gifts which become curses to
true love, he sees all that Ethel is doing, and
all that Ethel's mother is meaning for her.
He sees her drawn into the magic circle which
surrounds fiercely-aristocratic old Lady St.
Just, who from her heights of age and rank,
treats Ethel and Lord Marcus as boy and girl,
and thus gives them the opportunity of being
more intimate and familiar than they otherwise would have been. Though he does not
hear the words they speak, for the Bishop
beams at him at brief intervals, he can feel
the arrangements for future meetings that are

being made with her ladyship's cognisance and sanction. *His* Ethel will be riding and dancing and playing tennis with this young lordling, whom in his heart he is calling " an arrogant beast of a boy," in places to which he —Walter Gifford—will have no right of access! He sees it all now! Her mother's recantation of the cordial assent she had given at first to their engagement; the motive for making the effort to get the St. Justs and the Bishop to this garden party, in order that Ethel may get return invitations to the set in which Lord Marcus will revolve; the reason why always charmingly-dressed Ethel is more charmingly dressed than ever to-day—all these things are seen and understood by him with horrible distinctness, and summed up tersely in his own mind thus:

" The mother's a designing woman, and she'll try to make Ethel throw me over for that boy with a handle to his name; but I'll have a fight for her."

" I don't think you quite admit the force of my remarks? " the Bishop questions, suavely, at this juncture, and Walter Gifford ruins his chance of ever being called upon to assuage gouty pangs in the episcopal feet and legs, by answering bluntly:

" I didn't hear them, my lord."

" Papa, have you asked Lord Marcus for to-morrow?" Miss Templeton puts in, with a little air of eagerness, which is meant to show " the mere country surgeon " that he is so completely outside their circle that they can discuss social arrangements before him with the same freedom they feel before servants and inferiors generally.

" For to-morrow?" the Bishop asks, perplexedly.

" Yes, to dinner! don't you remember? Lord and Lady St. Just are coming and Mrs. Heatherley and Ethel."

Walter Gifford turns away sharply and hears no more. In another moment he has gained Ethel's side, and detached her from the aristocratic group who are seeking to absorb her.

" Ethel," he begins, a little too gravely, " why haven't you told me that you dine at the Palace to-morrow?"

"Really, Walter," Ethel says, with some of her mother's vivacity (vivacity which strikes Mr. Gifford painfully as being assumed); "really, Walter! *did* I undertake to tell you where I dined every day when we became engaged?"

"You put it in a way that makes me seem a petty tyrant, even in my own eyes; and yet I know I'm right and you're wrong the whole time," he says, wearily; and Ethel, quick to mark the change in him, has her hand on his arm, clasping it caressingly in a moment.

"Walter! don't look tired and disappointed, it hurts me; mother told me not to say anything about dining at the Palace, 'it would look like boasting,' she thought; and mother has such perfect taste and tact, now, hasn't she?"

"She has indeed! such perfect taste and tact that I feel I jar upon her at every turn to-day," he says, bitterly.

"No, you don't," the girl cries, with quick compunction; "only do be broad and look at things as they are, and not try to distort them into what you think they ought to be; be as friendly with Lord Marcus Boyne as he would be with you, and take it for granted, Walter, that *I* shall keep my promise as sacredly to you as I should do to a peer of the realm."

The girl draws herself up and looks proud and noble, true and trustworthy, to a degree that reassures him, as she says this. And for the hour Walter Gifford is satisfied that the idol he has set up will never prove false to him.

CHAPTER II.

THE BISHOP'S DAUGHTER.

TO do the Bishop justice, he would rather go without the dinner than give it to-day. And this, not because he is an ascetic on principle, but simply because his digestion is out of repair, and his bones are aching.

It is hard on him that these things should be, for he has lived sparsely for many a long year; and now that the good things of this life are about him abundantly, he does not dare to indulge in them, any more than if he had revelled in them from his cradle.

But his daughter has ordained this dinner; and what is socially ordained by Miss Templeton, at the Palace, is as the laws of the Medes and Persians.

At times she runs her social ways mysteriously, giving out an impression subtly that she has a deeper meaning hidden in her

virgin heart than is given out and suffered to
appear on the surface. If the Bishop utters
a faint protest against the expediency of
having a lawn-tennis party, when the clouds
are loweringly threatening rain ; or hints that
it would be pleasanter for him to defer a state
dinner until such time as there might be a
slight chance of his being able to eat some of
it, his daughter's reply invariably crushes out
all opposition.

" *I* have a reason for having it now, papa ;
you know I never do anything without a
motive."

To-day, Fanny Templeton has a very strong
motive for insisting on this dinner coming off
—a motive that, though not noble, is, at least,
essentially feminine. Her mature fancy has
been favourably affected by Mr. Townley's
handsome, aristocratic, gay-hearted young
pupil, and she desires to give him the chance
of reciprocating her flattering sentiments.
She has been a girl so long that she cannot
get out of the habit of thinking herself one
still, though she has had ten more years'
experience of life than Lord Marcus.

And, to be quite fair to her, the mistake of
regarding herself as a girl still, is a par-
donable one on her part; for if a woman is
only as old as she looks, it must be admitted
that Fanny Templeton looks very young
indeed. She is one of those fair, soft-looking
women, whose cheeks retain the roses and
roundness of youth well on into middle age.

She has, too, one of those coolly constituted
natures that never take it out of their pos-
sessors by giving way to deep or violent
emotions. Her blue eyes are not in the habit
of shedding tears, for no trouble worth crying
about has ever touched herself, and she is a
very heroine in the way in which she can
calmly contemplate the troubles of others.
Her father has been Bishop of Allerton Towers
for ten years now, and during these ten years
she has had no need to take depressing heed
to pecuniary ways and means. Additionally,
she has had thrust upon her a delightful sense
of social importance, and in small, soft ways,
social importance is very dear to the good
Bishop's daughter. Altogether, the circumstances of her life are rejuvenating, and she

is justified in feeling that, as far as looks go, age need be no barrier to the alliance she hopes to compass.

But Ethel Heatherley may be! Miss Templeton rarely deceives herself, whatever she may do to others ; and she admits that, whereas she is only a pretty young woman, Ethel Heatherley is a beautiful young girl, upon whom Lord Marcus Boyne has already bestowed very favourable glances. She recognises the fact also that if Ethel does enter the lists against her, that it will be a case of two to one ; for Mrs. Heatherley will be on Ethel's side, and Fanny Templeton is fully aware of the widow's value as an ally and dangerous qualities as an opponent. And these two are not the sole barriers between herself and holy matrimony with Lord Marcus.

The Bishop has a chaplain !

This fact, as an isolated one, is unimportant. Every Bishop has a chaplain, and frequently nature and Providence combine to make a union between the Bishop's chaplain and the Bishop's daughter a highly desirable thing. But in this case Fanny Templeton has come to feel that it would be, to say the least of it, unadvisable for her to throw herself away on a mere Reverend Bernard Grove, when it is in the order of things " that may be " that she shall become eventually the Marchioness of Monkstown.

It is true that " things have been," between Bernard Grove and the Bishop's daughter, which are not now. It is the fashion of smart leader writers, reviewers, and others of that ilk, to represent and pretend to believe that a curate is necessarily a rather effeminate, poor-spirited, mild-game-playing, weakly, flirting sort of creature. They heighten the obnoxious tones in which they paint this picture by sneering allusions to the impunity with which ladies, young and old, may " pet " the shepherd of the flock, and assume an idiotic air of surprise if a curate —" *a poor curate* " is the happy phrase to properly describe him—does anything that commends itself to the eyes of the world as indisputably manly. Why this idea should pervade the press-reviewing and ordinary fiction writing mind is incomprehensible to every one who mixes in decent society, and knows that the clergy are quite up to the level of not only "gentlemanliness," but "manliness," as exhibited by the members of any other profession, class,. or clique. Nor does the person who mixes in this aforesaid decent society find that the "poor curate" differs in any way from the "rich rector" in birth, breeding, education, or manner. But those who are outside the pale of good society do not understand or realise this truism. And so the innumerable vulgar men and women, who supply cheap periodicals with emotional stories of that life among the upper classes of which they know nothing, invariably portray "the curate" as a susceptible ass, or a scheming, hungry fortune-hunter, and make fatuous jokes about his goodness and poverty for the edification and amusement of the dissenting masses.

It shall be told at once that Bernard Grove is not a type of either of these classes. He is merely an honourable, good, good-looking, well-bred, and equally well-read gentleman. Poor enough, in all conscience, to satisfy the greedy desire of all those who would see the priests of the Lord impecunious. But neither mean-spirited nor threadbare, crawling nor audacious on the strength of his spiritual position. Only a gentleman! gifted with the grace of high culture and real religious feeling.

It is, however, with his social status and his social career only, that we have to do in these chronicles of life at Allerton Towers.

He has been the Bishop's chaplain for three years now; and other men, interested in the question, in the diocese, are beginning to say that his chances of a good living from his diocesan are going off rapidly. For Miss Templeton has visibly cooled towards him recently, and it is tacitly understood that the best living in the Bishop's gift will go to the successful clerical wooer of the Bishop's daughter.

Other chaplains had come and gone before him, but something had always intervened between themselves and the means of obtaining the coveted promotion. In two cases it had been a wife and several children. In another, a band of hopeless, helpless, penniless sisters. But Mr. Grove had come upon the stage free from all encumbrances, and the heart of the Bishop's daughter had gone out to him gladly. Unfortunately, as far as regards his chances of getting the best living in the diocese, he had not responded with flattering celerity.

But after a time, she, showing him her liking in a thousand undemonstrative ways, he, being only a man, began to be moved to regard her in the light of, at least, a warm and dear friend. The constant daily intercourse gradually melted the bulwark of indifference behind which he had found safety at first, and when once she had compelled him to feel that she was both pretty and pleasant, and, moreover, very partial to himself, the rest was easy.

It certainly would have ended in his marrying her, and thus getting that good living of which mention has been made, had not a check been given to the completion of the half-formed scheme by an unintentional outsider.

Things are in this state of check now, and have been ever since Lord Marcus Boyne came so blithely within the borders of Allerton Towers. For Miss Templeton is quite as well posted up in the probabilities of Lord Marcus succeeding to the title and estates of his father as Mrs. Heatherley is. Accordingly, the cool, well-regulated pulses of the Bishop's daughter cease to beat for the man who never can make her more than a rector's—perhaps a rich rector's—wife, and throb with amiably selfish tenderness for the handsome boy who can make her a marchioness.

Fanny Templeton is, perhaps, as cautious a girl as ever guided herself through the intricate ways of good society. But there are times when her over-caution, combined with that high estimate of her own charms which so nearly approaches vanity, betrays that which she most ardently desires to conceal

It is so now, and though she has never so

much as mentioned Lord Marcus's name to Mr. Grove, that gentleman knows as well as she does herself that the woman who was ready to be his wife only the other day, is now even readier to be the wife of the boy who has the pleasure-loving desire to taste all that is sweetest, as well as the brilliancy of the butterfly.

Mr. Grove sees and admits this, and is, to tell the truth, not very much piqued at it. His feeling for the lady, who has been using her womanly wiles to win him, is not sufficient for resentment to take the place of the liking she herself planted. Accordingly, he makes no change in his manner of treating her, with the kindly intention of showing her that he has no manner of objection to her carrying her new point—if she can! And she misconstrues this considerate thoughtfulness of his, and thinks that he is determined to consider their relations unchanged, and fears she may have some difficulty in getting rid of him without the shadow of a scandal should she succeed with Lord Marcus.

On the other hand, she does not deem it

wise to burn her boats. To be *quite* off with
the old love before she is on with the new, is
a weak policy according to her ideas. So she
puts her manner into the scales with her
chances, and as these latter go up and
down, so shall the former vary delicately
and safely.

It is grievous to Miss Templeton that the
Heatherleys should be here on this, the first
day of Lord Marcus's dining with them, but
it is better to have him with them than not
to have him at all. Besides, Ethel Heatherley
is engaged, and though she believes Ethel to
be quite as capable of being off with the old
love if a satisfactory new one appears on the
horizon as she is herself, still she will make
Lord Marcus feel that Ethel is devoted to her
lover, if the English language can do it.

Through the whole of the day she has
successfully evaded a *tête-à-tête* with Mr. Grove,
little suspecting that he has not made the
slightest attempt to have one with her. On
other sultry summer days, such as this, it had
been her wont after she has seen her housekeeper and ordered the domestic doings for

the day, to go out on the velvet lawn through which the river runs, and over which the grand cathedral casts its dignified shadow, and spend the hours till luncheon. For the Bishop's study window peeps out through an ivy screen upon this lawn, and when the Bishop and his chaplain have transacted their morning's business of seeing suppliant clergy, and answering a budget of supplicating, rebuking, or defiant letters from others, what more natural than that the younger man should get himself out into the fresh air under the waving trees, and glance through the magazines and new publications with which Miss Templeton always sedulously provides herself?

But the "old order changeth!" This morning there is no lady on the lawn ready to look up—with a smile playing over the softly-tinted rounded cheeks, and the prettily cut pink lips—at his approach. Nevertheless, Mr. Grove takes his accustomed seat with the air of one who is perfectly satisfied with things as they are, and reads a couple of stiff articles in *The Fortnightly* right through, without stopping to give one thought to the one who is fancying that her current course of conduct is giving him pain, and causing him bewilderment.

" When the time comes for him to know it, he shall not have it to say that I misled him for a moment after I began to care for Marcus," Miss Templeton says to herself, complaisantly ; and she really credits herself with holding rather exalted sentiments, and with acting in an irreproachable manner.

In the afternoon it is her custom to drive with her father for two hours, and often, when any of the country magnates are to be honoured with a call, Mr. Grove accompanies them. Indeed, the city of Allerton Towers itself is rarely honoured by the presence of its Bishop, and the city clergy are never invited to partake of the hospitality of the palace. Why this should be is not clear to the secular mind, which does not understand why this delicate line should be drawn between the cathedral and the city clergy, or why a faint show of the episcopal favour should be extended to the country rectors and vicars,.

which is withheld from their brothers in the
town. But, as Miss Templeton says of herself, she never does anything without a
motive, and Miss Templeton is the daughter
of her father.

On this exceptional day, however, Miss
Templeton does not second even with a look
the Bishop's suggestion that Mr. Grove shall
drive out with them to Collingham, five miles
from Allerton Towers, to look at a newly-
erected church which the Bishop is to con-
secrate during the ensuing week. On the
contrary, she puts on a look of filial solici-
tude, and exclaims almost tearfully against
the gentle exertion which her father is
contemplating.

"The effort of getting into this room was
almost too much for you this morning, papa,"
she says; and then, for the first time this day,
she lifts her lashes, and looks Mr. Grove in
the face.

"I am sure you agree with me that it
would be injudicious in the extreme on papa's
part to venture out, with his left foot swollen
as it is?" she says, appealingly; and Mr.

Grove replies with an air of good-humoured indifference that makes her fear he is going to obtusely disregard her change of feeling respecting him.

" I am sure that the Bishop can settle that question for himself; but as regards my going with you, my lord, I shall ask you to excuse me to-day ? "

" Certainly ; but I thought it would have been well for you to find out what they mean to do at Collingham on the fifteenth," the Bishop says, testily. The vicar of Collingham is believed to be as much in favour of ad-vanced ritual as his Bishop is opposed to it. And it adds to all the gouty symptoms, this lurking fear that his lordship has, that he may be surprised into sanctioning the coloured vestments and other things which are abominable in his eyes, if his chaplain does not reconnoitre the dubious ground beforehand.

" I think I may safely say that everything is sure to be done decently and in order at Collingham on the fifteenth," Mr. Grove says, speaking far too cheerfully and approvingly

of that local head-centre of good churchman-
ship, his broad Bishop thinks.

"I specially wished to go to-day," the
Bishop says, repiningly; and his daughter
puts in—

"Dear papa, don't you think it would be
better to keep away from Collingham till the
day? You can't stand altercation on any
subject, and if Mr. Harcourt means to make a
fight for certain things of which you so
properly disapprove, won't it be easier for
you to put it down with authority on the day
when your presence is essential, than to
quibble about it beforehand? I am sure you
think I am right?" she adds, turning—with
a pathetic look of reliance on his always
thinking her that, at least—to Mr. Grove.

"I think you're admirably prudent and
perfectly right if you wish to save the Bishop
from being troubled," Mr. Grove says, cheerfully; and again Fanny tells herself that the
"poor fellow is blinding himself to her change
of feeling, and that it will be a heavy trial to
her by-and-bye to make him understand that
she has altered." But even as she tells her-

self this, she cannot help seeing that Mr.
Grove is very unconcerned, not to say in-
different, about missing the opportunity of
driving with her this afternoon.

The end of it is that the Bishop, rendered
litigious by the absence of his chaplain and
the presence of his daughter, in an absent
mood, goes out to Collingham, and finds fault,
that he feels to be uncalled for, with most of
the arrangements which the vicar has made
for the fifteenth. So the pebble thrown into
the social pool, innocently enough, by Lord
Marcus Boyne, is making rapidly widening
circles.

Out on the lawn while they are away this
afternoon, the chaplain sits reading, and now
and again reviewing the situation.

"Poor old fellow!—he hasn't been taught
yet that I am to be petted no longer," he half
laughs to himself, and then for a few minutes
he does seriously consider whether or not
Fanny Templeton is the kind of woman whom
it would be well for him to make his wife?
After a brief period, he says, with an air of
relief, "Well! she has settled it easily for me,

as it happens; it might have been, if it hadn't been for this young fellow's opportune appearance: as it is!—I hope, for old time's sake, she won't make a fool of herself: Marcus Boyne is a mere boy, and will regard her as an old woman."

When the Bishop and his daughter come back from Collingham they find Mr. Grove ready to welcome them with unusual impressiveness.

"Such capital news I have had by the five o'clock post," he says, with animation, "my old friend, Colereigh, has been offered a colonial Bishopric — Fitz-Spitzburg — somewhere up the South African diamond fields, I fancy; he's coming over to see me before he goes: I shouldn't wonder if he wants me to go with him."

"They're giving these colonial bishoprics to the wrong men," the Bishop says, testily, "we ought to send out men of moderate views, not those who offer themselves as violent contrasts to those of us at home who like to go on quietly, and are averse to ceremonial."

"Some of those at home go on so quietly

that the heathen might be forgiven for imagining that sleep and sloth in religious matters were the things needful," Mr. Grove replies, and Fanny says, hastily—

"Missionary work would suit you I'm sure; you like roughing it and opposing people; now for my part I feel that I could only be good in an atmosphere of peace."

("She fears I may ask her to go with me, poor girl!" the chaplain thinks.)

Lord St. Just takes Miss Templeton in to dinner this night, in the order of things. He is a pleasant old gentleman—when he has been kept away from strong waters for some hours—full of scientific information, which he is willing to impart to anybody who listens to him with appreciative understanding, but rather apt to relapse into a grimly-smiling, and silently-ironical frame of mind, when his words of wisdom are not waited upon. This is the case now, for on Miss Templeton's other side is Lord Marcus Boyne, separated by some two others on the same side of the table from Ethel Heatherley.

"He shall not even see her during dinner,"

the astute hostess has declared; "and I shall interest him sufficiently to make him come to me instead of to her in the evening."

If Miss Templeton were quite candid she would confess to herself that by "interesting him" she means that she hopes "to disgust him with Ethel," by speaking of the latter's engagement to Mr. Gifford, "one of the town surgeons."

CHAPTER III.

"I SHALL NEVER FORGET YOU; NEVER!"

"IT was touch-and-go whether I came to-night or not; I'd made an engagement, before I had your invitation, to go with some fishermen, and see what they call a seine drawn: I forgot that, you see, when I said I would dine here, and to-night I forgot I was coming here, and was going off with them, when Mrs. Townley charged at me with a rebuke and a reminder."

Lord Marcus makes this unflattering confession with a candid coolness that disarms Miss Templeton's resentment. It is not a difficult task for a woman who wishes to be a marchioness to pardon a small slight from the man who may make her one.

"Oh! it's so dangerous going out with the seine; I should have been dismal all the evening if you had forgotten us for the fish," Miss Templeton says, pathetically.

" I wouldn't regret the fish for a moment, if you had put me next to, or opposite to, that lovely Miss Heatherley," he replies, ungratefully.

Miss Templeton presses her lips a trifle closer together, and lowers her eye-lashes for a moment. Then she lifts the cloudless, blue eyes with a smile, and says:

" Perhaps you would have found her even a duller companion than you are finding me, she is not like the same girl she was before her engagement; so dreadfully engrossed with thoughts of the absent love, that she is almost useless now in society."

" It is not really an engagement, is it?" Lord Marcus asks, kindling to the topic.

" It is, indeed, a real engagement, and it will be quite a love match, in spite of all her mother's machinations," Miss Templeton laughs. " Poor Mrs. Heatherley! her own day is done, and she may easily be forgiven for being a *little* disappointed at Ethel's having fallen so desperately in love with a man who hasn't much of a home, and no position whatever to offer her; but Ethel will have her own way in this as in other things."

Lord Marcus fixes his sparkling eyes on her, with a serious expression in them, which gives a new charm to his boyish, handsome face, and is—silent.

There is a little awkwardness in renewing the conversation, as he will not aid her; but she is equal to the task, for she has a few more shots to fire.

"For my own part, I am glad it is settled so, for I am very fond of Ethel," she begins, looking fondly down the table at Miss Heatherley's profile. "I'm very fond of her, very; but she has been such a silly little, easy-dazzled, little flirt, that it is a comfort to know she is settled at last with a man who is able to take care of her."

"I think she can take care of herself."

Miss Templeton laughs and shakes her head.

"She's only a little rustic after all, you know; poor Mrs. Heatherley gives herself dreadful airs—to a great extent, I fear, because we have noticed them a good deal—but Ethel knows nothing of society; if it had not been for this marriage (Lord Marcus winces) I should have had her in town with me next season——"

"What a stir she'd have made," he murmurs with enthusiasm, "she is prettier than the prettiest woman I saw at the princess's ball just before I came down, and all the beauties who are in the best swim were there."

"It will not be much use for a country surgeon's wife to make a stir in the 'best swim,'" Miss Templeton says, coldly. Then she remembers Lord St. Just's claims on her, and tries to give her undivided attention to him for five minutes, hoping that Lord Marcus Boyne will feel punished by her neglect.

Lord St. Just has taken sufficient wine at this juncture to make him feel bitter about having been debarred from speaking of his favourite hobby for so long a time. Accordingly he is not in charity with anyone, least of all with the man who has been preferred to him by his one socially legal auditor.

"Is that young fellow as witless as his

brother Kenmare, that you have to waste
so many words in making him understand
that he's not to cast his eyes at pretty Miss
Heatherley," he says, sardonically, and Miss
Templeton could eat him as she feels that
Lord Marcus hears the speech and is amused
by it.

" Pretty Miss Heatherley is so hopelessly
attached to her rather rough hero, that I have
no need to caution Lord Marcus against
falling into the pit which her ambitious
mamma is quite prepared to dig for him,"
Fanny says, presently, and Lord St. Just
gnashes his teeth and smiles, and compliments Miss Templeton on that " well-known
engineering skill which will doubtless enable
her to undermine Mrs. Heatherley."

All this time she has nearly forgotten Mr.
Grove, who is down at the other end of the
table, near enough to the Bishop to come to
the rescue should his lordship unwarily fall
into any theological difficulties. There is a
good deal of excitement frequently about this
task of extricating the Bishop, for he is apt
to forget, at times, that he has solemnly

pledged himself to the rigorous observance of
certain forms and ceremonies, which occa-
sionally he denounces as "puerile, childish,
popish, and altogether abominable." The
duty of figuratively picking his lordship
up, setting him erect before the Church and
the world, and saving him from falling into
unconscious heresy, is ofttimes a hard one.
But Mr. Groves does his best to perform it,
and his best is the work of a churchman, a
gentleman, and a peacemaker.

He has been having a hard time of it
during this dinner, for Collingham is on the
tapis, and the Bishop, supported by some recently delivered judgments, is as a lion on
the subject of one or two things that will
give him extra trouble if he does "not stamp
them out," as he vehemently expresses the
operation he proposes to himself. To revise,
cancel some portion of, and generally edit,
the Bishop during the heat of a controversy
into which he has hurled himself unsupported
by facts, has been a task for a Titan. But
Mr. Grove has not only undertaken it, but
actually carried it through.

And all the while he has been in this fray, Miss Templeton deludes herself (when she has time to think about him at all) with the idea that he has been aching and seething at the sight of his successful rival on her left hand.

They go into the drawing-room presently, and Ethel instantly finds her way to a deep old bow window, with cushioned seats in its recess, in a corner of the room. She takes up her position without let or hindrance from Fanny Templeton, for this window is remote from the piano and other points of general attraction in the room, and the girl, engaged as she is, will not have the face to seclude herself in such a corner with a man, Miss Templeton thinks.

Fanny has found out that Lord Marcus is fond of music, and sings and plays a little himself. It is a terrible trial to her now, that she should have disregarded the efforts her music and singing masters made in years gone by, to instil something like artistic feeling into her; for, intuitively, she feels that Lord Marcus will not listen tolerantly to mere namby-pamby prettiness, such as she can deliver. With a further pang, she reflects that Ethel Heatherley plays the violin, and plays it well, too, for an amateur! Blessings from Miss Templeton for her own far-sightedness in not having asked Ethel to bring her violin to night.

In a short time it all seems to be going as Fanny wishes. Old Lady St. Just has got Mrs. Heatherley well within her gossiping clutches, so that there is nothing to be feared from the widow, as regards the Bishop, yet awhile. Mr. Grove is discussing the possibility and advisability of making an underground railway right into the heart of Dartmoor; thus rendering access to the most picturesque points easy, and at the same time preserving the wild aspect of the place unimpaired. Other people have grouped themselves together more or less uncongenially and incongruously, and Lord Marcus is safely landed at that bane to peace in the majority of houses—the piano.

"Mrs. Townley tells me you have such a lovely voice, and such a perfect style," she says; and he laughs buoyantly.

" Mrs. Townley knows little of music and less of styles. My voice is good enough as far as nature goes, but I haven't had much good training."

" But you will sing something to oblige us? It will be *such* a pleasure to hear you! Oh, *do !* "

She begins to pick a number of songs out of the music-stand, but he repulses her, and refuses them politely.

" Haven't learnt one of them, Miss Templeton, and wouldn't offend your ears by crudely singing anything I hadn't learnt," he says, gallantly; but she knows that he is looking about for Ethel as he speaks. Suddenly he discerns Miss Heatherley, and crosses over to , her leisurely, quite regardless of the expression of mingled spite and admiration in the blue eyes which follow him.

" Will you play an accompaniment for me?" he asks, gently; "'Twickenham Ferry;' you know it."

" Yes, I know," she says, rising swiftly, and coming out of the mysterious light of the recess with a bright gladness in her face and manner that undoes all Miss Templeton's work. "I wish I had my fiddle here," she goes on, as she seats herself at the piano, " it *goes* with the violin, oh! so deliciously."

She seems half appealing to Miss Templeton for an endorsement of her sentiments respecting her beloved violin, but that lady's heart is hardened towards her.

"A little bird has whispered to me that Mr. Gifford wishes your choice had fallen on any other musical instrument than the violin, Ethel; how will he like your speaking of it as 'your fiddle?'"

Ethel turns slowly to the piano, draws off her many buttoned gloves without the slightest sign of haste or annoyance, flutters her small, nervous hand over the keys, and looks up into Lord Marcus's face with a smile for which Fanny could kill her.

"Now!" Ethel says; and the pleased. enamoured young fellow sings " Twickenham Ferry," to her sympathetic accompaniment, in a way he has never sang it before—or since!

They all listen to him, and to her—spellbound, till the last echo of the last whispering notes die out; then a chorus of thanks and admiration greet both the brilliant young performers.

In listening to the thrilling strain, the Bishop has forgotten Collingham and his gout, but both are rapidly recalled to him when his daughter crosses over, and whispers:

"There is nothing in the song itself, but the way *her* playing prompted him to sing it was simply shocking! Speak to Ethel, papa, for her own sake; point out the impropriety of that daring, defiant style; and don't hint to her that I have asked you to do it, or the poor, vain, silly child may think I'm jealous of her."

So, at the bidding of his exemplary child, the good Bishop presently calls Ethel to his side, and unwillingly reproves her.

"It's a dreadful song for that boy to have sung in the Palace, before me," he says, as austerely as he can bring himself to speak to the pretty widow's prettier daughter, " and I'm sorry to find that you are so well acquainted with it as to be able to play it in a way that must have shocked everybody."

"What harm is there in the song? I'll ask you about my playing the accompaniment afterwards," Ethel asks, respectfully; but there is a light in her brown velvet eyes, that shows she is ready for battle.

"No actual harm, but it's altogether not quite the song for a lady or gentleman to sing in a drawing-room before other ladies and gentlemen."

"Ladies and gentlemen listen to it delightedly at concerts."

"In private society it is not well that the full meaning should be put either into the words or air," the Bishop says, dictatorially; and then, satisfied that he has said enough to satisfy his daughter and his conscience for the present, he resumes his conversation with the Townleys, and leaves Ethel to reflect on his counsels.

Humming the last two lines of the song which has been the cause of her disgrace, Ethel saunters away to her seat in the window again, and there, behind the curtain, is Lord Marcus.

"I didn't see you come," she says; and he

knows there is no girlish subterfuge here; she did *not* see him come.

"Isn't it the best place in the room?" the girl goes on, never lowering her voice a half-tone, but speaking out so that all in the room may hear if they be minded to listen. "The view is lovely, and we needn't talk."

She plants herself on the low seat opposite to him, and he crosses to her side quickly.

"It *is* the best place in the room, for it's the place you're in; and I can't look at the view, lovely as it is, while I can look at you; and as for one not talking, I must say something to you. May I?"

"You say 'you must,'" she says, looking at him with wonder in her eyes.

"Well, I must. It is this: I shall never forget you, never! And you are engaged?"

"I am engaged to Mr. Gifford; I told you that myself, yesterday," she says, looking at him too kindly.

"And yesterday I heard, and didn't care whether I believed it or not; to-night I've heard it again. It was dinned into my ears all through dinner, and now I can't bear to believe it. Do you know why?"

"Because you like me yourself, I suppose," the girl says, proudly; "that's the only reason I can think of, and I'm sorry."

"Oh! Ethel, it's because I love you," he says, bending nearer to her — worshipping her with the pure worship of a young man's first passionate love--"don't be sorry for me, whichever way it goes; be glad, for if I ever can gain you it will be my life's happiness, and if I'm to lose you! Well! be. glad I have loved you, won't you?"

"You'll forget me and your fancy in a week," Ethel says; and she tries to say it steadily, and tries to believe that she means it.

"Forget you!" He rises up, and stands before her straight, erect, beautiful in his youth and strength, and love for her.

"Forget you! Is it because I'm younger than the man in whose love you are going to rely that you think mine will fade? or is it because you despise me for having been so quickly won, that you think I shall be lightly lost?"

"No; it's because I love the other one best that I say you'll soon forget me; because I hope you will."

"Best! Then you do feel something— liking or something for me?" he pleads, eagerly; but before Ethel can answer him, Miss Templeton dances into the recess, and puts her hand within Ethel's arm.

"I hope the others—the Townleys especi-ally—haven't noticed this, Ethel," she whis-pers, and the grip on Ethel's arm grows vicious as she says it. Then she adds aloud to Lord Marcus:

"Mr. Townley has said good-night to us, and the carriage is at the door; do you go with them?"

"No. I shall walk home to-night," he says, gloomily.

"Walk! impossible! it's five miles. Stay here, my father will be most happy if you will, I am sure; if you are determined not to drive."

"Thanks, Miss Templeton, but to stay here

would be more impossible still; in the first place I have no clothes with me, and in the second place——"

" What? "

" I have no inclination—to stay without them," he says, lazily; and then he takes Ethel's hand, and mutters "good-night" to her.

" Good-night, good-bye," Ethel says, rather chokingly; it is a bit of romance, and she rather likes it. Still she thinks it would be well to end it!—while yet there is time!

" It isn't ' good-bye,' " Lord Marcus says, impetuously; " it can't be that—when you're the *one* person in the world I want to see again."

He wrings her hand, and something in the strong grasp impresses her with the truth and reality of what he has been saying to her. And she cannot but be pitiful towards the man who has given his love to her so unreservedly and quickly, and to whom she feels convinced she can never give her love in return.

As soon as he is gone Miss Templeton drops her mask of sweetness.

" Ethel!" she begins, in a tone of reproba-
tion ; "you have been more than foolish to-
night ; even papa spoke of the way in which
you played just now, so professional and
showy, not at all what we could have wished
to hear in our drawing-room ; and then, to
cap such an exhibition, you retire into a
dark corner with a young man who is a
stranger, and flirt with him in a way that
must have amused him."

Ethel's eyes flash in the growing darkness
—" Don't call me 'Ethel' when you speak to
me in· that way, Miss Templeton, or rather
never speak to me again till you can remember that I am neither your dependent nor
your servant, but your equal ; and as for
your father's opinion of my manner of playing, you worded it for him, and made him
say it, because you knew Lord Marcus sang
the song as if he loved it simply because I
played it for him."

" Oh, Ethel!" Miss Templeton cries, desperately, feeling that if she has driven Ethel
into open rebellion, the girl will hold no
terms, will keep no covenant.

"I am 'Miss Heatherley' to you, if you please, until you tell me you are sorry for having insulted me," the girl cries, passionately. "Wasn't it bad enough to be tempted——"

She checks herself abruptly, walks like a queen into the lighted room, and bending over her mother, whispers, " We have stayed too late, mother dear ! come ! "

CHAPTER IV.

IT is the morning after the dinner at the Palace, and Ethel Heatherley is out in the garden at the back of her mother's pretty cottage, alone with thoughts that are not pleasant.

She cannot help admitting to herself that she did like that brief, spasmodic bit of romance which flashed into her life so unexpectedly on the previous evening. She liked it at the time, and remembers it with blushes and pride, and pleasure now. And for doing this she knows she ought to be thoroughly ashamed of herself, for the man whom she is pledged to marry has announced that he is coming to have a serious talk with her this morning, and he is not the man who has temporarily glorified existence for her with this flash of bright romance.

"I shall never forget you, never!" she

keeps on repeating to herself, but, do all
she can, she fails to utter the words with
that drawing sweetness which had been in
his tones when he uttered them. Did he,
could he mean them? She hopes not; for
of course she is engaged to Walter, and she
loves him dearly, and wouldn't do anything
but marry him for the world. Still, did
Lord Marcus mean them?

Marcus is a lovely name, too, she tells
herself. His name, Marcus Boyne, attracts
her more than his title, it's so Irish, and so
uncommon, and so exactly the gallant-sound-
ing, fitting name for so gallant-looking a
hero. *How* he rang out those words—

"With love like a rose at the stern of the wherry,
There's danger in rowing to Twickenham Town."

What an old prude the Bishop was for carp-
ing at such a sweet love-song. But no! it
wasn't the Bishop's fault, poor old man; it
was Fanny who had prompted her father to
find fault; it was Fanny's jealousy, the
foolish, spiteful thing; as if he would ever
look at her, even if she, Ethel Heatherley,
didn't exist.

Was he fickle, as Irishmen are, prover-
bially? Would he forget her, as she had
told him he would in a week? How she
would like to test him, and find him faithful
and true ; that is to say, how she would like
to do it if Walter (dear, good Walter, who
shouldn't be snubbed for anyone) didn't exist;
and Walter was coming in a moment, and
Lord Marcus had said he would " never forget her, never ! "

" She looks prettier this morning than she
has ever looked in her life, and somehow
or other she knows that she does so, and
attributes this pleasing result rather to the
effect of the new emotions which have been
awakened in her by the brief romance of last
night, than to the deliciously-tinted pale pink
lawn dress, with its flounces and frills of
white lace. New feelings, new emotions, new
aspirations, new possibilities have entered in
and taken possession of and beautified her,
all through this bright glimpse she has had
of an ardent's man's suddenly-developed admiration and love.

If he could only see her this morning he

would surely like her better than ever. *If he could only see her!* Not that she wishes him to come, or to see her, or to think about her any more; but he had said he should " never forget her, never; " and after that, what can she do but think of him a little, for a time at least.

She is startled out of her meditations on this head abruptly, by a step close to her side, a hand on her shoulder, and a voice in her ear, saying,

" Ethel, darling, I'm afraid I've kept you waiting, but I've heard from my sister, offering to come and stay with me; she wants to come at once, and to bring a friend with her, so I've been about searching for lodgings, and the time has slipped away without my knowing it."

He stoops over her as he speaks, as if to kiss her, but Ethel stands a little aloof, not angrily, nor coldly, but just as if a kiss from him were not in the programme at the moment.

" I didn't know you were late. I mean, you haven't kept me waiting," Ethel says, hurriedly, and then, seeing that Mr. Gifford looks hurt and surprised, she tries to throw a little extra interest into her next words.

" I'm so glad your sister is coming, Walter, it will be so nice for you. But why are you getting lodgings for her? Why won't she stay with you?"

" Didn't I tell you she is bringing a friend with her?"

" But why can't the friend stay with you, too?"

" The friend is a young lady, and it wouldn't be quite the thing for her to stay in a bachelor's house."

" What nonsense! What utter nonsense! Not the proper thing to stay in a bachelor's house, when the bachelor's sister is with him. Such prudery and rubbish! I've no doubt she's an old maid whom you wouldn't look at ; besides (with a gay, self-satisfied laugh), while I am in the way she needn't be afraid of your falling in love with her, need she?"

" She's not an old maid," he says, with slight embarrassment.

" Isn't she?" Ethel asks, quickly. " You

told me your sister is twenty-nine or thirty, so I took it for granted that her friend would be equally aged. What is her name? Is she pretty?"

" Very," he says, emphatically.

" Oh!"

" Very pretty, and very clever, and——"

" How pleased you must feel at the prospect of welcoming her," Ethel interrupts, with a little air of hauteur that becomes her well, and that pleases Walter Gifford, because he fancies it betokens jealousy! Alas! for him and his short-sightedness. Ethel's jealousy will never bring her nearer to him. His first instinct against the coming of his sister's friend has been a correct one. Her presence will bring no peace to him.

" I am not at all pleased, to tell the truth. I wish Mabel had come by herself, and then she could have stayed with me ; as it is, Miss Somerset has spoilt the pleasure of my sister's visit, as far as I am concerned."

" Don't you like Miss Somerset?"

" My not wishing her to come has nothing to do with my liking, or not liking her. I'm annoyed because she will take Mabel into lodgings instead of letting her come to me, and she will engross my sister entirely."

"You either hate or love her very much, Walter," Ethel says, gravely. "I wonder which it is?"

"It certainly is not 'love' that I feel for the lady who is going to interfere with my plans for Mabel."

"Then it has been love, now, hasn't it? If she is less than a friend to you now, it is because she has at some period in the past been more than a friend. Won't you trust me and tell me, Walter? I shouldn't be the least bit annoyed or hurt. I'm not silly enough to fancy that I am the only one you have ever cared for. One can't have one, and only one love in a life——"

"I hoped that I was your first love, at any rate, Ethel; and told myself that I had won you utterly."

"You shouldn't tell yourself anything so foolish and dog in-the-mangerish. Why should I only have the pleasure of being in love once, any more than the rest of my fellow-creatures? You've half confessed already, at least, I've screwed it out of you, that you *have* been in love with this Miss Somerset, whatever you may be now. Why should I be different, and vow truly that you're the first and only one my heart has thought of for a minute?"

"If I could think you were jealous," he is beginning, when she laughs and stops him.

"No, no, Walter! I'm not jealous, I'm only glad to find that I'm not so much, so everything to you, as I thought I was; it would have frightened me to feel that you never had loved anybody, and never could love anybody but me; now I feel freer, oh! ever so much freer."

"I'm sorry that your assumption of facts, that you can't verify, should give you such liberty of conscience. Miss Somerset is no more to me than any other person who intervenes between me and unfettered intercourse with my sister."

"You got red about her," Ethel says, with a lively laugh, that seems to tell him she does not care whether he is in love with Miss Somerset or not.

"I came to speak to you about something widely different, and that is your mother's unjustifiable opposition to our engagement, after having given her free consent to it."

"Don't call anything my mother does or says 'unjustifiable,' if you please."

"It is unjustifiable to profess perfect satisfaction with a man and his prospects one day, and then, suddenly, without any change having taken place in either, to find fault with both."

"Mother doesn't find fault with you, as a man."

"She does with my position, and seems to distrust my power of improving it; and you don't appear the least distressed at her doing so. Why is this, Ethel? What has happened to change you from the dear, loving, devoted, staunch little girl you were that day you said you would be my wife?"

"Please don't use such words and such grand sentiments about it," Ethel says, with unaffected distaste to the subject; "you're

making it all big and important by the way
you speak! Why can't you let things be?
Why can't you drift on just as we are, con-
tentedly, for a little time?"

"Because I love you, Ethel, and can't see
you either taken from me, or drifting from
me, without showing the pain I feel," he
says, with emotion.

They have come away from the house,
down along the winding paths that lead
from the pretty, old-fashioned garden to the
banks of the river, as he says this; and now
they stand in silence for a time, looking down
at the water, as it ripples and leaps now
along quiet places, and now over big boulders.
On the opposite side of the river, the Palace
grounds spread their stately, sheltered walks
and lawns, and, presently looking across,
Ethel sees, on one of these latter, Miss
Templeton sitting on a rustic bench, under
a deeply-drooping tree, looking down com-
placently at a manly form reclining on the
grass at her feet.

"Fanny and Mr. Grove don't often come
. so far as this," Ethel is saying, when the

manly form starts to its feet, with an amount of activity that does not characterise Mr. Grove's movements usually, and a strong, clear, young voice calls out,

"Hold hard, there, will you, Miss Heatherley, and I'll cross over on some of these big stones," and Ethel recognises the form and voice of Lord Marcus Boyne, and cannot restrain an exclamation of glad delight as she does recognise him.

This at the first blush of pleasure! A moment after she remembers that Lord Marcus can never be anything to her, and that her lover is by her side! Oh! the joy there *ought* to be in such a reflection! Oh! the flat pain there *is* in it !

("That puppy here again!") she hears Mr. Gifford mutter, and she can't refrain from saying,

"He's manly and gentlemanly, and bright and beautiful! Why do you call him a 'puppy,' Walter?"

"'Beautiful!' What a word to use about a man! One gets a contempt for the man to whom it's applied, even if one hadn't it before."

"Why?" Ethel asks, impetuously, as she eagerly watches Lord Marcus's perilous passage across the boulders, over which the river is rushing tumultuously. "Why? We use it about a sunset, and a horse, and a mountain; why not about a man?"

"Pshaw!"

"There's no argument against its use in *that*, anyway," Ethel says, stubbornly. Then she drops her acknowledged lover's arm, which has been holding her tightly this while, and goes off to meet the unacknowledged one, as he clambers up the bank, flushed and dripping from his exploit.

"A modern Leander!" Miss Templeton shouts from her dry and deserted position on the opposite lawn; but her spitefully suggestive words fall on Walter Gifford's ears only, and deeply do they aggravate him. The others hear them not. Ethel is bending over the bank, holding an enthusiastic hand out to Lord Marcus, who is leaping up in most Leander-like fashion, quite oblivious of the jealous glances which are being hurled at them from either side of the bank.

" I have come to tell you something," Lord
Marcus gasps, as he reaches level land. " I
know you won't care to hear it, but, still, I
can't help wanting to tell you, and to hear
you say you're sorry for me. Kenmare—
he's my brother, you know ?—is awfully ill,
and I'm going home at once to see him ; but
I wouldn't go without saying good-bye to
you."

He is holding her hand, and looking into
her face with his wonderful, glistening, aqua-
marine eyes, and she is tenderly touched, as it
behoves a woman to be who hears of the
sudden illness, which may possibly have a
fatal termination, of one who is dear to one
whom she loves.

" Perhaps your brother will get better,"
she blurts out, prosaically ; " but, if you
wanted to say good-bye to me, why were you
lying on the lawn at Miss Templeton's
feet ? "

" Because I had to take a message from
Townley to the Bishop ; and when I said I
was coming on here to the cottage, she told
me she expected you there this morning,

and said I should miss you if I didn't wait. Would you have been sorry? Would you have cared a bit, Ethel?"

"Ethel," Mr. Gifford shouts from a height a few yards above her, looking down with threatening eyes upon the fascinating, frivolous pair. "Ethel, I must go in five minutes, and I have many things to say to you."

"Why the deuce doesn't he say them and have done with it," young Marcus Boyne mutters to himself, discontentedly. He is mad with fate, love, everything this morning! and Ethel's eyes are distracting him. Why are the "sweetest eyes that were ever seen" predestined to light the path of another man? Why may he not dare to ask her to definitely break all previous bonds, and share his fortunes with his heart to-day?

No, he cannot. There is that man on the little winding path above them proclaiming his rights in the cold, cavilling, displeased tone in which he says—

"Ethel, I must go in five minutes."

Wearily, Ethel begins to ascend the winding

path. What is she to say to Walter Gifford when she rejoins him? Nothing; absolutely nothing! She cannot thank him for waiting for her, for she has not wanted him to wait! She cannot profess to think that he will be glad to see Lord Marcus Boyne, because she knows that the young man's name is as the root of bitterness to him! And if she does not do either of these things, Walter may be righteously annoyed.

"Why, oh why, has any one but mother the right to control me or find fault with me?" she says to herself, as she plods up the path, Lord Marcus affectionately at her heels. Then she meets Walter Gifford, and must say something.

"You don't know one another, I find? Mr. Gifford, let me introduce you to Lord Marcus Boyne; now come in and see mother," she adds, with an air of relief, turning towards Lord Marcus.

"And you stay here with me," Walter Gifford puts in, decisively.

She looks from one to the other for a moment, and then makes up her mind that she cannot even *seem* to slight the man who is in sorrow about his brother.

"Lord Marcus's will be rather a sad goodbye, Walter," she says, gently; "you are going to see your sister and her friend, who are both full of spirits and life; he is going to his dying brother. I think I must stay with him and mother."

Walter Gifford stands back and folds his arms over his chest. In that moment he comes to a definite conclusion concerning the part he will play in this drama. Ethel shall go her own way for a year. At the end of that year he will either have the power to control her, or the will to resist her! What matter which? She shall go her own way now.

"It must be as you please," he says, inclining his head, and Ethel lifts her bonnie, blooming face towards him and answers—

"My pleasure is that you go and enjoy yourself with your sister and Miss Somerset, for a time, and leave me to mother! Now, you can't say *I'm* nasty, and exacting, and jealous."

"I wish to Heaven you were," he says, piteously, but she is not listening to him. She is already running up the winding path, with Lord Marcus by her side.

The young Irishman has all his woman-worshipping wits about him, for all the real trouble he is in about his brother.

"I knew it was on the cards that you couldn't or wouldn't see me if I came," he says, with that bewitching humility which more than other form of pride compels a woman to surrender; "but still, I thought I'd come and ask for your sympathy, though you can't give me your——"

"Oh! don't, don't." They are in the clematis-covered entrance-porch to the cottage now—a little place—the interior of which is a mass of tea-roses, stephanotis, gardenia, and giant mignonette. It is all so sweet that for a few moments poor Ethel feels sweetly astray. Then she recovers herself.

"I wish Mr. Gifford had come with us," she says, rather mournfully.

"If he had I shouldn't be here now," Lord Marcus cries. Then he goes down on

one knee before her, and she can but hear
what he has to say.

"Ethel, I love you, I love you; whatever
comes, I shall come back and tell you so;
Ethel, you are my star! Guide me back to
you soon; forgive me for saying this now
when he's here, and I oughtn't to say it, but
I'm unhappy about my brother, and I want
someone to love me. I mean I want to tell
someone all about myself and what's before me."

Ethel is leaning back against a shelf, her
hands behind her, tightly clasping it, and he
is standing before her, grief-stricken, be-
wilderingly handsome, and utterly oblivious
of the fact that the man she is pledged to
marry is standing a few yards away from
them, anathematising him.

In response to his ardent appeal, Ethel,
with the instinct for self-preservation which
is inherent in her sex, says nothing; but
moves discreetly towards the inner hall,
cooing out as she moves,

"Mother! mother! we want you! Are
you not down yet, darling?" and presently
Mrs. Heatherley appears, all India muslin

and surah, and soft laces, looking her freshest, sweetest, airiest morning self in fact, and, as with a quick glance she takes in the whole situation (for Walter Gifford is looming gloomily in the background), Ethel feels that the onus is off her!

"Mother will manage them both," she says to herself, with a sensation of relief, for it has not come to the pass yet, with her, that she desires to manage either of them apart from "mother."

"My dear boy," Mrs. Heatherley says, quiveringly, presently, when she has heard the reason why he has been recalled home, "my heart bids me go and help to nurse your brother; but my motives might be misconstrued if I volunteered for the service! What say you? Shall I go?"

For a moment Lord Marcus thinks of his motherless, dying brother, away in the imposing but exceedingly ill-regulated Irish castle, and is half inclined to accept the Quixotic offer. The next he looks at Ethel's face, and reads her look of pained, scornful disapproval aright.

"I daren't ask you, though I'd give all I have, or may have, in the world to get you and Ethel there," he says, with unwonted trembling and hesitation in his voice and manner. And Mrs. Heatherley looks at him with tears of maternal understanding in her eyes, and Ethel turns away hastily, and gets out to look for Walter Gifford.

He is just about to depart when she comes, and it is in his heart to punish her for having been so long.

"I had a hundred things to say to you, Ethel; but you have been so much taken up with Lord Marcus, that I must put them off till the evening."

"Or till another day—say till you've found lodgings for your sister and Miss Somerset," she says, calmly.

"Ethel! don't send me off like this! and don't be dazzled by that boy."

"That 'boy,' as you call him, is not in the 'dazzling' line of business, at present. He's in grief, *real* grief, about his brother Kenmare.'

" If Kenmare dies, he will be the Marquis. His grief is as real as all else about him," Walter Gifford storms out ; and Ethel can only say,

" Walter ! how can you say it ? "

CHAPTER V

ENTER LILY. EXIT ETHEL.

MORE than a week has elapsed. Mr Gifford has found the most comfortable and picturesque lodgings for his sister and her friend that the heart of woman can desire, or the most exacting and fastidious nature of man can desire for her.

Three lavender-scented rooms in a sweet farm-house, called "The Uplands," are placed at their service by one of the bonniest-faced housewives in the West counties.

Three old, raftered rooms, low and roomy, with quaint corner cupboards full of china, and long, queerly carved settles along the walls. Rooms that are full of the sweetness and light of the country, and, it may be told here, rooms into which Lily Somerset would rather die than enter, if she too had not an end to gain.

For she is one of the world's spoilt darlings, and for her "to rough it" in ever so slight a degree, is an extraordinary thing.

It is the morning after their arrival at the Uplands—the farm-house that lies on the breezy borders of Allerton Towers—and the two ladies are sitting at their rather late breakfast, in the old oak-panelled, low-raftered sitting room which has been placed at their service.

Anything more incongruous than these two friends are in appearance, manners, motives, habits, and aspirations, cannot well be imagined. Mabel Gifford is a tall, stout, good-humoured, commonplace-looking woman of thirty, full of thriftiness, and excellent household ways, blessed with an eagle's eye for the main chance. Not a mean woman! Far be it from the chronicler of this portion of her blameless, uneventful career, to suggest that Mabel Gifford is endowed, in ever so slight a degree, with the quality of meanness. But essentially a thrifty, careful, saving woman, who, abhorring every form of luxury and extravagance for herself, is rather apt to be intolerant of it in others.

Yet, see her now, the chosen friend and companion of Lily Somerset, a girl of four-and-twenty, whose fortunes are as fair as her most lovely face—a girl who has never known what it is to deny herself anything that money can purchase, or which she has set her heart upon having—a girl to whom fine raiment is absolutely one of the chief necessaries of life, who invariably averts her eyes from the seamy side of everything, and who feels it rather hard that some one cannot bribe the sun to perpetually shine upon her—a self-indulgent, wilful, capricious, extravagant, exacting, ungrateful young lady, yet one for whom Mabel Gifford is willing to sacrifice her time, principles, occupations, sharply-defined rules of life, and personal independence.

She does not puzzle her head much by trying to define the reason why she has gone into this bondage to one who, she feels dimly, will cast her off and do without her very buoyantly as soon as she no longer needs her. It is enough for Miss Gifford, who has no charms, no caprices, and but a very narrow fortune of her own, to shine in the reflected light of this glittering fairy queen, who is as fair, slender, graceful, and sweet to look upon as the lily whose name she bears.

Miss Somerset is lying back in the most comfortable chair in the room, her long morning gown of cream Madras muslin and lace floating away in soft folds around her fragile figure. Her beautifully shod diminutive feet are stuck up on a chair in front of her. A cup of chocolate is frothing on the table by her side, and Miss Gifford is just engaged in the critical task of selecting the daintiest bit of sweetbread in the dish, wherewith to tempt her (Lily's) fitful appetite.

"Put your hat on, Mabel, and go at once," Miss Somerset is saying, after there has been a short pause in the conversation.

"Yes, dear. Go where?" Miss Gifford replies, acquiescently, but vaguely.

"To your brother, of course. Oh, I forgot you didn't know what I have been thinking about. I have just made up my mind that I won't touch a thing, not a single thing, for breakfast, until I know what Mr. Gifford means by treating me in this exceedingly rude manner."

"Rude, my dear! Walter *rude* to *you!* He couldn't be."

"It's bearish of him not to have come to inquire for me this morning, after that hideous journey yesterday; and I will not be treated with churlish discourtesy by any man, least of all by Walter Gifford. He must come, and make something like an apology to me, before I touch anything this morning; and if I go without my chocolate, I'm always ill, as you know; so go at once, please."

Mabel Gifford rises promptly, and puts on her hat; but she sighs as she does it, for she knows that her task is a hopeless one, and that when she comes back with it unfulfilled, her loved tyrant will make her suffer for her inability to perform it.

"You must remember that Walter's time is not his own," she says, feebly.

"Then pray who's is it?" Lily retorts, imperiously.

"Well, a doctor, you know, must consider his patients before even his friends," Miss Gifford says, humbly.

"I will not have his patients considered

before me, and he would never be fool enough
to tell me that he does so," Lily says, with
smiling derision.   "You are blundering, as
usual, you good, awkward old Mab, in your
efforts to defend your brother; you had much
better simply do as I tell you—go and tell
him he must come at once.   Leave the work
of explanation to him."

It is in Miss Gifford's mind to say, "Time
was when Walter would have left every
patient in the world for your sake, and then
you drove him from you."   But she does not
say it, for it is the fondest desire of her heart
that these two shall come together again, and
she humbly acknowledges that she is not
gifted with the grace of uttering those seasonable words which may bring this desirable
end about.

The young surgeon's house is in one of the
most picturesque quarters of the old city, but
the distance between it and the Uplands farm-
house, where the two ladies are lodging, is as
wide as Walter has been able to make it.
His sister's feet grow tired, and her soul grows
sad as she walks it rapidly this morning, for

she detects a meaning in his having placed them so far away.

"He doesn't want to be in the way of seeing her often, I'm afraid," Mabel soliloquises, shaking her head. "And I really do believe, now, that she's got to be fond of him, and finds she can't do without him; what a thing it would be for dear Walter. Five thousand a year, and no one to interfere with the way she spends it! There'd be an end of all the working and scraping and toiling, and being beaten back by richer men, who can afford to make more flourish about what they do, if Walter will *only* love and trust her again."

Walter is just coming out of his surgery door, into the yard, where his stanhope is waiting for him. The stanhope "looks prosperous," Mabel thinks, for it is well built and well kept, and the big, powerfully modelled bay horse that stands between the shafts has a satisfactory air of sleekness about him, that reassures his owner's sister. Still! "It is hard work, grinding work, for poor Walter to keep things up to the mark, I know," his sister thinks, pityingly, as she steps across the

yard towards him. Then in a moment it
flashes across her, that he may be Lily
Somerset's husband, and the master of five
thousand a year, if he pleases, and her pity
resolves itself into a sensible, practical, earnest
desire and intention, to see that he uses this
opportunity aright.

"You moving at this hour, after your journey, Mabel," he says, addressing her in cheerful accents, though he has no cheerfulness in
his heart, for he has not seen Ethel since that
day when he left her pouring out pity, that
seemed to him misapplied, for Lord Marcus
Boyne, about his brother Lord Kenmare.
How, therefore, should cheerfulness and himself be "on terms" just now?

"Yes, Walter, and I'm here without having
had any breakfast, let me tell you," Mabel
says, querulously, and then, as she sees that he
is about to step into his stanhope, she makes
a sudden step forward, lays her hand on his
arm, and arrests his further progress.

"You must come back with me, Walter.
Lily is—is *hurt* that you haven't been over
already; you'll come back with me now?"

Walter Gifford slowly takes out a note-book of imposing proportions, and reads a list of cases and the hours which he is bound to give to them.

"You see, Mabel, I have no time to give to you this morning," he says, as he closes the note-book.

"Not to me, but to *her*," his sister pleads with unconscious pathos.

"Nonsense, dear old girl." He speaks with affected unconcern and indifference, but within he is terribly moved. Why cannot this Syren cease to lure him now, when he is so nearly safely anchored in a far more holy love? Why cannot she cease to strive to distract him? Why—cannot she cease to be herself, in fact?

"Nonsense, dear old girl; my time is not my own. Present my compliments to Miss Somerset, and tell her that if she gets bilious or neuralgic down here, I will come to her at once, in pursuit of my calling; but while she is well and happy, she does not need me, and other people do."

He steps up into his stanhope as he speaks,

and his sister imperils all her limbs in striving
to follow him.

"But, Walter! do listen!"

Brightly he leans forward, holding the
reins, and looking horribly ready to drive
over her, she thinks.

."I am listening."

"Think, Walter; think of what I shall
have to endure when I go back without you!
Lily is nervous this morning; take her as one
of the patients whom you will not neglect."

As his sister says this, Mr. Gifford thinks of
Ethel, the girl he loves and longs to marry;
of Ethel, the girl who seems so heartily disin-
clined to marry him just at present. Then
across the thought of her, comes another
thought—a thought, lightning-like, of Lily,
who is all flush and glow, and passionate
resolve!

"With all my heart, I wish Miss Somerset
had selected another spot to recover her
faded health in, and another medical adviser
than myself; understand me, Mabel! I will
not help Lily out in another sham! tell her
so from me."

"If I dared to do it, she would be sitting in your surgery when you came home to-day. Walter, be sensible, be led by Lily and me."

"Led! to what?"

"To be what you wanted to be once to her. Oh, Walter, do listen, think of her beauty, and sweetness, and money; think!"

"Of their all being the devil's snares for me, and of how I won't be snared," he said, coldly; "go back to your friend, Mabel, and tell her that I know now what self-preservation means; I shall not leave my duty at her bidding."

"And she won't touch a bit of breakfast till she sees you," Mabel pleads, as she sees the chances of her mission ending successfully fading away.

"Then I fear she will not breakfast to-day," he laughs, "for when I come back from my rounds, I am due at Mrs. Heatherley's."

"Who is Mrs. Heatherley?"

"She is Ethel's mother, and Ethel is the girl I hope to make my wife."

"Walter!"

" Why this announcement? "

" I have never even heard of her."

" No ; I have kept my heart's darling very close," he says, meditatively.

" Are you teasing and trying me? I hope you are, Walter, for rather than go back and repeat what you have just said, as a truth, to Lily, I would—I don't know where I wouldn't go."

" Come up and have a quiet talk with me this evening, Mabel," he answers, for his sister's manner and appearance is too flustered and heart-rending altogether for him to hold further converse with her now. A strong, brawny woman dissolved in tears is a sight to make even strong men shudder and depart from it ; they themselves being the cause of the unseemly emotion being the more cogent reason why they are intolerant of it.

" If *this* is what I have come to Allerton Towers for, I could almost wish I had stayed at home, though for months it has been the dearest wish of my heart to see you, Walter," Miss Gifford says, half to her brother and half to herself, as he drives away, and leaves her in the full morning light, clearly outlined and very warm, in his stable yard.

Presently, stepping daintily and tenderly across the paving stones, there comes a delicate little lady, vaporously dressed in raiment of the most gossamer-like grey. Intuitively, Miss Gifford feels that this is an antagonist, and when with a pardoning smile the transparent intruder addresses her, the substantial sister feels that Walter's path may be beset with other snares than his own untoward will.

" *Has* Mr. Gifford gone? Ah! how unfortunate I am, to be so late," the pretty little lady in grey exclaims, disconsolately, and a conviction starts through Mabel's mind, that this can be no other than the Mrs. Heatherley to whom Walter has declared he is due as soon as he has finished his rounds.

" My brother is gone for several hours, I believe," Miss Gifford says, frigidly, and Mrs. Heatherley, with eyes wide open with perplexity and friendly feeling, murmurs:

" Your brother; is it possible? I am delighted to meet such a sister of Mr.

Gifford's, for I take a deep interest in him, and have so often wished that he had a wise sister near him."

"I am the only sister he has, and I am near enough to him now," Mabel says, fluently. "As to my wiseness! we won't say about that at present—as you are such a friend of Walter's, I may venture to ask your name."

"Oh! I am Mrs. Heatherley," the fair little widow says, with the prettiest air of surprise imaginable. That anyone should be ignorant of her name and status, is not at all in order at Allerton Towers.

"Ethel's mother!" Miss Gifford cries, surprised out of prudence, and Mrs. Heatherley nods her head assentingly, and says:

"Yes, Ethel is the name of my child, and now you have come, I almost regret that I have just made arrangements for taking her away for a time; she is so young, and as it is so terribly dull here, at last I have yielded to her unspoken plea for a change; we leave Allerton Towers just as you come to it, Miss Gifford; can anything be more unfortunate?"

Mrs. Heatherley does not even assume the shallow appearance of being sorry for the combination of circumstances which she is verbally regretting, and Mabel Gifford feels her face flushing with mortification. That Ethel's mother is no more anxious for the engagement to last and the marriage eventually to come off, than she herself, Walter's sister, is, is evident to her, and it angers her that it should be so. She can justify herself for undervaluing and lightly regarding the unknown Ethel. But that Mrs. Heatherley should presume to undervalue Walter, whom she knows, goads Walter's sister into the utterance of words of indiscretion.

"I have just heard something from my brother that makes me feel rather surprised at your daughter's desire to go away from Allerton Towers," Mabel says, stiffly; and Mrs. Heatherley aggravates the already aggravated sister still further by taking no notice of her remark.

"When did you say you expected your brother home? I am most anxious to see him before I go, in order that he may pre-

scribe for my neuralgia. You would hardly
believe it, Miss Gifford, but I am a martyr to
my nerves——"

"My brother will be home in the course of
two or three hours," Mabel interrupts. "Are
you leaving so suddenly that you won't wait
to see him?"

"The train will not wait for us, my
dear Miss Gifford," the little widow says,
graciously; "we leave in an hour, I regret
to say, as I should *much* like to have seen
Mr. Gifford, so kind and nice as I have always
found him; but the train, like the tide, waits
for no man, you know, and the hour is fixed
for us to join our friends the St. Justs, at the
station; delightful people, Lord and Lady
St. Just; I wish your brother knew more
of them. We have arranged a little tour
together. My Ethel is enthusiastic about
scenery. If we had been staying here, I
should have begged you to be kind enough
to come to the cottage and look at some of
her sketches! as it is, unfortunately, all I can
say is, good-bye, dear Miss Gifford, and I
trust we may meet again."

Bewildered and annoyed as she is, still Mabel has no definite ground of offence against Mrs. Heatherley, and cannot, therefore, refuse to take the graciously proffered little hand which that lady extends.

"But it seemed to sting me, Walter," she says, by-and-bye, when she is reporting the interview to her astonished and aggrieved brother, who has not seen Ethel for a week!

"Ethel, gone! without a word to me! Impossible!" he says, sternly. But when he goes up to the cottage to have the "mistake," as he believes it to be, triumphantly rectified, he finds the place deserted and its occupants flown.

The servants are "left in charge, on board-wages, for six weeks at least," they tell him; but they cannot give him any address, as missus said "there was no need to forward letters; everything would keep till she came home."

He has a sharp tussle with his pride for a few minutes, and then he asks:

"Is there no note, no message for me, from Miss Heatherley?"

"Not a line, nor a word, sir," they tell him, cheerfully; and his heart is aflame with wrath and fear. Instinctively he feels that Mrs. Heatherley is going to try the well-known power absence has of making the heart grow fonder of—somebody else; and his jealous fancy vainly strives to paint the lucky man who will be fiendishly invited to join the party by that atrocious old match-maker, Lady St. Just.

"And, unless Ethel writes to me, I can't send her a line, praying her to be staunch," he tells himself, miserably; "her mother has planned it well! I can't combat that false little fairy, who looks as innocent as a hare-bell. She has planned it well! And she will teach Ethel to think me careless and in-indifferent."

There is no professional call on his time this evening, and in his desolate, miserable dulness he is more than half inclined to go to the Uplands, where two women are wait-ing to welcome him with warm gladness, in sharp contrast to the two who have gone away from him with callous indifference. But he

subdues the half inclination, telling himself
that he will be a true knight to Ethel, however sorely she may try him.

It is disappointing after this to find his
sister and Miss Somerset waiting for him
under the verandah, outside his drawing-
room window.

CHAPTER VI.

ETHEL HEATHERLEY must be freed from the odium of being suspected of being either heartless or sly with as little delay as possible. The temptation of being taken into the heart of beautiful scenery has been put before her suddenly and adroitly by old Lady St. Just, who likes interfering with a love-affair for love of inter-ference; and who, additionally, really thinks "that pretty Ethel Heatherley ought to marry someone better than a country surgeon." Having once committed herself to the public statement of this opinion, she is determined to leave no stone unturned in the path by which she proposes to lead Ethel out of the local difficulty; and, without consulting Ethel's feel-ings or wishes in the least, proceeds to pull various strings, by means of which she intends to set various influential puppets in motion.

"Keep her from corresponding with the young man while she is away, and leave the rest to me," her ladyship says to Mrs. Heatherley, "and be ready to start within an hour after Ethel hears that we are going."

"All letters shall wait our return, and I'm always in light marching order," Mrs. Heatherley says, blithely. "My only difficulty will be in case she insists on seeing him before she goes."

"Don't let her know she's going till he has started on his long morning round. The rest will be easy. Ethel is not an infatuated goose. She won't be impolite enough to want to make us lose our train, in order that she may take a sentimental leave of her lover," Lady St. Just says, gruffly. And on these lines Mrs. Heatherley works.

Ethel is apprised of the contemplated pleasure-trip, made to engross herself with packing, told of Miss Gifford's arrival with a "lovely friend, who has already shocked the worthy mistress of the Uplands by her eagerness to see Mr. Gifford," and, in short, admirably "managed" through the hour that elapses between her hearing that she is to go, and her going.

When, in a flush of pleased excitement at the prospect of the change, mixed with a blush at the sound of the alarming charms of Miss Somerset, Ethel comes down ready dressed for the journey, Lady St. Just is waiting for them in her carriage at the door.

"Mother," Ethel whispers, "you *said* you'd go and tell Walter, and fetch him up. Have you been? Why isn't he here?"

"His sister was there, dear child, and I could not get a clear answer from her as to where her brother was," Mrs. Heatherley says, with affected hesitation. "Don't mind it, dear; if he's worth anything, he will *not* be dazzled away from you, though they say this Miss Somerset is *very* dazzling. I almost wish I had not sent up to the farm for eggs this morning; then I should not have heard of her beauty, and her anxiety to see 'Walter,' as she calls him. The servant told Sarah that the young lady wouldn't eat any breakfast till Miss Gifford went to fetch her brother; so, I suppose, he had gone to the Uplands when I went to his house with your message. Naturally, I did *not* leave it with his sister."

Mrs. Heatherley speaks almost sadly, her sympathy with her child is so strong. But her heart bounds with delight when Ethel replies :

"Come, mother, dear ; Lady St. Just is waiting for us. Walter will write to me, if he cares still. Of course, he'll get our address from the servants."

This is not said in the form of a question ; consequently Mrs. Heatherley does not feel called upon to answer it. In a few minutes her heart bounds more exultantly still ! They are clear out of Allerton Towers without having met with any obstruction from Walter Gifford. It will be six weeks before he will have a chance of making a personal appeal to Ethel ! Time is so kind in the way of obliterating one set of impressions, and substituting others. Ethel is so pretty, and fascinating, and sensible ; and dear Lady

St. Just is so practical and successful as a
social diplomatist! No wonder that Mrs.
Heatherley feels satisfied that these ensuing
six weeks will contain all the possibilities
on which she relies to save her.

"It has all been so sudden that I don't
even know where we are going first," Ethel
says, as the train bears them free of Allerton
Towers.

"Be satisfied to know that Lady St. Just
has arranged a series of most delightful
surprises for you, Ethel. You could never
have arranged anything half so charming
for yourself," her mother says, rapturously:
and Ethel strives to express gratitude, and
to repress curiosity. But the latter is very
strong within her, and will put forth its head
again presently.

"Shall we be travelling all the time, Lady
St. Just?"

"We shall travel till we settle for a time,"
her ladyship says, and again Ethel combats
curiosity successfully for a few minutes.

"Shall we settle for more than a week?"

Lady St. Just nods assent.

" For a fortnight; or a month perhaps ? "

" About a month; that will bring us to the end of September, and the best of the shooting will be over then."

" Oh ! Are we going to stay at a shooting box ? "

" Yes."

" At one of Lord St. Just's ? "

" At one he rents."

" Where is it ? "

" In Gloucestershire."

" Lady St. Just, do tell me a little more about it; I've never been at a shooting box; is this one large or small, beautiful or bleak, and what is it called ? "

" It's a bijou shooting box, and it's called Boyne Gate," Lady St. Just says, fixing her eyes full on Ethel. " If you want to know more about it, my dear, you must get your information from the Marquis of Monkstown, of whom we rent it, when he and his son, Lord Kenmare, come to stay with us in a fortnight."

Ethel feels her face tingling as this abrupt mention is made of Marcus Boyne's father

and brother; but she struggles to speak
unconcernedly :

" I thought Lord Kenmare was very ill? "

" The one you are thinking of died the
day before yesterday; Marcus is Kenmare
now. And now, my dear, take your book,
or keep quiet; I like to read when I'm
travelling, and hate to be bothered with
questions."

Ethel is only too glad to avail herself
of the opportunity of hiding her confusion
under cover of being engrossed with a
book. Has Fate played her this trick, and
are her mother and Lady St. Just guiltless
in the matter of bringing her into collision
with that delightfully dangerous rock on
which her fidelity to Walter Gifford was
so nearly wrecked the other day? If Fate
alone is to blame, then will Ethel go
through the ordeal of another meeting
with Marcus without repining and without
reproach. But if her mother and Lady
St. Just are leagued against her and Walter,
then Ethel will retire from the unequal
battle, lest she loses it.

"Oh, Walter! pray that I may be true if I am tried," the girl says to herself, " for I love you and honour you; but the other loves me so well, and tells me, too, so warmly."

Meanwhile " the other "—his sorrowful duty of soothing the last sad, nearly un- conscious hours of his afflicted brother over —is trying hard to reconcile the conflicting influences of his father and his unwon love.

The young man's task is a hard one. He is Lord Kenmare now, the heir and hope of his house, and his father can but partially conceal the satisfaction he feels in having such an heir. The Marquis of Monkstown has suffered keenly both in his affections and his pride during the whole term of life allotted to the poor boy who is now gone. He has loved him, Kenmare, as a son, but he has shrank with bitter sickening pain of mind and heart from the thought of Kenmare as his successor. And in a dim way the poor young fellow, who has not been so altogether witless as some have believed, has felt and mourned over his own indolent inability to satisfy. When this grief and mourning and self-distrust has been overwhelming him at times, he would have died under it, battered down by the hard heavy cruelty of it, had it not been for his brother Marcus. But Marcus is too like the mother they loved and have lost, to have anything but deep generous love in his heart for his brother. So it is in Marcus's arms that Kenmare has died, and to Marcus's lot it falls now to bear the brunt of the first burst of mingled grief and relief which emanates from Lord Monkstown, carrying with it a confidence which is almost a command.

"While my poor boy lived I said nothing to you about your cousin Caroline; your uncle would never have let her look at you," Lord Monkstown says to the son who is Lord Kenmare now, and who will be Marquis of Monkstown, the day after the death which Marcus is deploring with boyish honesty and fervour; "but it's different now, and it's my duty as a father to tell you what good fortune may be yours for the asking."

"I think there's only one human being

on the face of the earth for whom I care
rather less than I do for my cousin Caroline,
and that is for my uncle Hawtrey," Kenmare
says, languidly. His thoughts are with his
dead brother and his living love, Ethel
Heatherley, " who will be sorry for his
loss when she hears of it." He does not
like having these thoughts rudely disturbed
by suggestions about relations whom he
rather dislikes than otherwise.

" Caroline Hawtrey has fifty thousand a
year of her own," Lord Monkstown says.

" Ah ! so I've heard ; she has reason to
bless Cotton. I suppose she'll buy a title
with it; something bigger than her mother
succeeded in getting. Sir John Hawtrey
was quite a little one, but he's a more
decent article to hand about as a father,
than old Willesdon, of Manchester, is re-
puted to have been."

" Sir John Hawtrey is your mother's brother, Kenmare," the Marquis says, rebukingly,
but his eyes kindle with sympathetic fire
when his son flashes out—

" A brother who gave my mother many a

heart-ache, many a rude rebuff and harsh word when she was Lady Kenmare, and some of his bloated wealth might have made life smoother than it was then for you and her. My brother, perhaps, would not have been afflicted as he was if his mother's brother had been more of a man and less of a mean brute before your eldest son was born, sir."

"Forget old injuries, Kenmare; Sir John and I have been friendly now for many a long year; we buried the hatchet——"

"When you came to the title and a good property; yes, I know that, father; but my brother's case was beyond medical skill by that time, I've heard my mother say, and when Sir John Hawtrey sheds crocodile tears over Kenmare's grave, I shall remember and perhaps remind him that the nephew he professes to lament might have been alive and well now, if he had spared a few guineas from his thousands some years ago to a sister's prayers and tears."

"Forgive us our trespasses as we forgive them that trespass against us;" quotes Lord Monkstown, gravely and earnestly, laying his hand on his son's shoulder. " Besides," he adds, " in any case she is guiltless of all offence against us. She must not be held accountable or to blame for her father's indifference and neglect. You are in a position to ask for the hand of any woman in England ; your uncle will admit that, though his daughter is a magnificent match from the money point of view, you will bestow a grand equivalent on her ; and as you are free to make it, I pray you to do so, my boy, for Irish land no longer keeps up Irish titles."

" I'm not free to make it," Kenmare says, quietly. He has grown considerably older during these sad days which he has spent by the bedside of his dying brother. Manhood and boyhood are separated by so fine and delicate a line that a sharp touch of sorrow, a keen feeling of responsibility, are, as a rule, quite sufficient to break it.

" Not free ! " Lord Monkstown has bushy eyebrows and penetrating deep blue eyes. His glance stabs like steel as he utters these words—" Not free ! "

" Well, not free in a sense," Kenmare says,

moving uneasily under the stabbing glance, not from any feeling of shame for his love, but because of the disquieting doubt he has of having won anything like reciprocal feeling from her.

"In what sense, may I ask, are you—who are responsible now for the honour of the house and the welfare of the house—bound?" the Marquis asks, with his grandest, because it is his most subdued and intensely quiet manner.

"I am neither bound nor free," Kenmare says, trying to laugh away his own confusion. "The truth is, sir, I have seen a girl who seems to me to be the only girl I can ever care to marry, but I am afraid she will never care to marry me."

"May I ask whether or not you have confided these romantic sentiments to the young lady?"

"I have let her know that I like her—that I like her better than any one else in the world," Kenmare says, flushing hotly.

"And she, I presume, has been prudent enough to say nothing definite?"

"Why should you presume that, sir?" Kenmare asked, angrily.

"Because I assume that you declared yourself—while you were my second son— with no income worth mentioning; it is to the credit of the girls of this generation that they are prudent enough to be indefinite with younger sons."

"She is not a girl of the class you are thinking of, sir!"

"Good Heavens, Kenmare, I am thinking of gentlewomen of our own class! Is your enslaver beyond that pale?"

"She is the sweetest gentlewoman that ever breathed," Kenmare cries, hotly; "but she is not a fashionable girl who regulates her smiles to the fellows about her according to their incomes; the same day I told her dear old Ken. was dying, I told her that I loved her and would go back to her; and she stood out against me, and tried her best to make me feel that nothing should ever tempt her to——"

He pauses abruptly; after all, he is not justified in speaking of Ethel's engagement to

Mr. Gifford, to his father, who will regard it as another insurmountable barrier to the accomplishment of his own (Kenmare's) wishes.

"Yes! that nothing shall ever tempt her to do—do what?" Lord Monkstown asks, icily.

"To—to have anything to do with me," Kenmare stammers out, composedly, and Lord Monkstown smiles in a weary, pitying way, that shows he suspects his son is not stating the case fully.

"I will not ask you to tell me this young lady's name; it is probably one I have never heard, nor will I ask where you met her; Townley ought to have known better than to bring you in contact with designing rustic beauty; however, as things are, all is well, and I am happy to find that I can honourably repeat what I said of you just now— you are free to make the best match that may be made in the kingdom; I need not add, my boy, that it is the fervent prayer of my poor, over-tried heart, that you make it."

"Does Miss Hawtrey know of your wishes?" Kenmare asked, gloomily.

"What are you thinking about?" Is it likely that we would risk wounding her *amour propre* until we were sure of your prompt and eager acquiescence in the scheme for your own happiness. Caroline will accompany her father, and when they leave we shall go back with them; Boyne Gate is close to Hawtrey's place, and I have accepted an invitation from St. Just to stay there for a month; by the way, Lady St. Just hopes that you will go to her for a few days."

"Hate staying at Boyne Gate," Kenmare grumbles, little guessing who will be there to make Boyne Gate an Elysium on earth to him.

"When you're tired of it you can go to your Uncle Hawtrey's, and in her own home you will have the best opportunity of studying the best way of winning my dear little niece," Lord Monkstown says, conclusively; and for the time Kenmare feels that it will be wise on his part to say no more of Ethel.

The poor young fellow feels the iron entering into him whichever way he turns. On

the one side is Ethel, who, though she has
not disdained, has unquestionably not en-
couraged his suit, and on the other side is
his father unconditionally scorning him for
pursuing it—or rather, for wanting to pursue
it, and despising Ethel without knowing
her.

"Jove! she'd match him for pride, and
beat him hollow for *savoir faire*," Kenmare
tells himself. At the same time he admits
to himself that his father will have a fair
amount of right and justice on his side
even if he does oppose an alliance with the
Heatherleys with all his might.

"The girl is perfect, as perfect as my wife
ought to be," the young fellow says, proudly
to himself, "but I wouldn't like to meet the
mother in the dark if I had offended her;
she'd as soon throttle that young doctor now
as look at him—for the sake of clearing my
path; and if an eligible duke cast a gracious
glance at Ethel!—the woman I want to make
my mother-in-law would gladly poison me!
All the same, I'll risk the surgeon's life and
my own for Ethel's sake."

CHAPTER VII.

THE travelling has been very pleasant, pleasant as only wealth and experience can make travelling, and, while it has lasted, Ethel has scarcely been conscious of missing anything; for the girl is still young enough and fresh enough to find happiness in mere change of scene; and, moreover, she has been the pet of the party. All things have been made to mould themselves to her wishes, and the feeling of consequence this course of treatment has engendered has been very delightful to her.

Two or three people who were not in the original programme have joined the party at various places. The Bishop and his daughter ran against them as they sauntered through a Surrey village one evening, in a way that would have surprised Lady St. Just and Ethel much less than it did if they had only known

that Mrs. Heatherley had written to the
Bishop three days before, hinting that a
rencontre with him in this very place would
be one of the happiest incidents of the tour.
This bait would, she well knew, be quite
sufficient to catch his lordship, were it not
for his daughter. That young lady being
capable of interfering successfully for the
salvation of her parent, if free herself, it was
necessary to hang a tempting bait out for
her also, therefore, Mrs. Heatherley threw
a September fly for her, and landed her
cleverly.

"I am sure Miss Templeton and you will
both be glad to hear that poor Lord Kenmare
has sufficiently recovered from the crushing
effects of the grief he felt at his brother's
death to promise to join us at Weybridge,
and, after a few days spent there in sketching,
boating, and fishing, to go on with us to
Boyne Place," the pretty little widow wrote,
laughing to herself the while, and telling
herself that "dear Fanny will leap at this
bait, and will bring dear papa to my feet
without delay, rather than lose the oppor-

tunity of displaying her pretty innocence
and disinterestedness to Kenmare in the midst
of river scenery! Let her come! He will
never even see her when my Ethel is by."

So they are at Weybridge now, spending
the late August days very happily, according
to their respective lights. Lady St. Just, who
really loves Ethel Heatherley for her frankness
and good looks, loves sketching also, and is
well satisfied to sit for hours in one of the
exquisite glades on St. George's Hill, while
the young folks roam about, and lose themselves in the wood, or to float idly in a boat
on the broad bosom of the Thames, while
Kenmare teaches Ethel how to hold her
line, and takes the little roach and barbel
off her hook, with a lingering tenderness
that is a maddening thing for Miss Templeton to witness.

For Fanny does not do herself the injustice
of absenting herself from any of these
lounges through the wood and on the river,
and, to her surprise, Ethel never seems to
wish to rid them of her (Fanny's) compan-
ionship. The Bishop's daughter is fairly

puzzled by this toleration, and is vexedly uncertain whether it is attributable to indiffer- ence to Kenmare or contempt for her own charms. But whatever it may be, she takes advantage of it to the utmost, and gives them all to understand that "dear Ethel can't bear to be a moment without her." And as Ethel does not take the trouble to contradict this statement, or in any way to tone it down, Ken- mare is compelled to take a part constantly in a trio while he is pining for a duet.

To tell the truth, Ethel is almost glad of the girlish vigilance which protects her from an outspoken avowal from Kenmare. For she is tempest-tossed in her own soul now by reason of the doubt of him, which Walter Gifford's continued silence is causing her to feel. And, worse than the silence, is the rumour which every now and again floats past her unwilling ear, relative to the beauty, and bewitching charms and caprices, and the lavish liberality to the poor, of Miss Somerset, "the doctor's sister's friend."

There is much of the happiness of "stolen joy" in this period to Kenmare. He has joined them at Lady St. Just's bidding, and his father is well pleased that it should be so, for every day the Marquis hopes to hear they are at Boyne Gate, in Caroline's atmosphere. An additional source of peace and satisfaction to Lord Monkstown may be found in the fact of his utter ignorance and unsuspicion of Miss Heatherley being the girl for whom his only son's heart is sick.

His son has not kept him in the dark as to the names of the other guests of Lady St. Just. With a half-sense of its being better to be. ingenuous than secret, Lord Kenmare has written: "There are three or four people here who seem to mean staying on at Boyne Gate. The Bishop of Allerton Towers, an old chap who would always be Vicar of Bray, and who promotes men of power and promise in his diocese without regard to their views, provided they can serve him when promoted; and his daughter, a girlish young creature, who means, I fancy, to be Lady Kenmare; Grove, the Bishop's chaplain, a right good fellow, and Mrs. Heatherley and her daughter. Mrs. H.

means the Bishop, as decidedly as the Bishop's daughter means me, and if the latter goes on neglecting her home policy on the chance of widening her borders and annexing me, she will find herself liberally endowed with a step-mother before she has time for protest or resistance."

"The governor can never say that I have kept Ethel's being here dark," Kenmare tells himself boldly, as he finishes writing this letter, which carries the happy conviction to his father's mind that "the boy is safe enough with the St. Just set."

But though Kenmare tells himself that he is putting himself beyond the reach of reproach by writing thus, his conscience tells him that he is acting disingenuously to say the least of it, if not deceitfully, in throwing his father off the right track by his mention of the Bishop's daughter, and mere cursory allusion to Miss Heatherley. It is in vain he tells himself that he has written nothing but the truth. He knows that he has suppressed the only part of it which holds vital interest for his father.

The hotel at which they have temporarily established themselves in Weybridge is down close by the ferry. You have only to saunter a few yards along the road, turn a corner round a hedge, and you find yourself on a slope of grass, with the broad shining river running along at your feet.

The silence and the beauty of the scene are very conducive to sentiment, especially by moonlight ; and by moonlight· Lord Kenmare strives to teach the full beauty of it, and of all the possibilities it suggests, to Ethel.

They are come to the very last August days now, and the harvest moon is nearly full. Dinner is over, and the elders of the party have settled themselves to the work that so speedily brings its own sweet reward, of peeling peaches and pouring out the wines that best assimilate with the subtle flavour of the fruit. The young people have strolled out, nominally to look at the effect of the moon over the extreme tip of the highest chimney-pot. When they have admired this exhaustively, a suggestion floats in the air as to their going down to the river, and Ethel and Miss Templeton act on it at once.

"We ought to follow the ladies and see that they come to no harm," Lord Kenmare says to Mr. Grove, and the latter immediately assenting (though at the same time he practically remarks that "the ladies are safe enough"), the quartette presently stand on the bank looking out at the ferry.

Suddenly the boat glides close up to them, and without giving a thought to the consequences, Ethel slips her hand out from Miss Templeton's restraining arm, and reaching a step forward, cries:

"Let us cross over to the other side, do? Who will come with me?"

"You must not think of it, Ethel," Fanny says, assuming the duenna demeanour far too naturally to be in keeping with the youthful *rôle* she desires to play. "Papa won't like it, and I'm sure Lady St. Just——"

"Mother won't mind my going, I know that," Ethel laughs. "You had better all three of you go back and proclaim that

you have no part with disobedient me. I
mean to go over."

"And I mean to come with you," Kenmare
cries, jumping into the boat, and drawing
Ethel after him, and in an instant the ferry-
man pushes off. Perhaps he feels that the
young pair in the boat are not dependent
for their current happiness upon the other
pair on the bank.

Miss Templeton's delicate pink cheeks grew
rosier even in the cold moonlight.

"Did you ever see such an audacious girl
as Ethel Heatherley?" she exclaims; "drag-
ging Lord Kenmare away alone with her in
this way; her conduct would be bold and
disgusting even if she were not engaged, as
it is it's disgraceful beyond everything."

"It was not Miss Heatherley's doings that
the boat pushed off without us," Mr. Grove
laughs; "she wanted us all to go, if you
remember; it is Lord Kenmare who has
seized the opportunity."

"The opportunity! for what?"

"For being alone with the girl he loves."

"Nonsense! she compels him to pay

her attention by flirting at him abominably, but I am *sure* he's not serious," Fanny says, sharply; "I could tell by the way he looked at me as he got in that he wanted me to go too; but I am not in the habit of doing such things," she winds up, lamely.

"I think you're mistaken about his having wished you to go with them," Grove says, simply; and then, without having the slightest desire to mortify her, but just because it is the case and he knows it, he adds:

"I saw him slip a coin into the ferry-man's hand, and heard him whisper 'Shove off.' I wish him success with Miss Heatherley, with all my heart; she'll make a splendid little marchioness and an equally good wife."

Miss Templeton shivers as she hears her own fears and suspicions confirmed in this way, and a gnawing desire to put herself beyond Lord Kenmare's reach should he even yet repent him of his evil ways and want to reach her, takes possession of her. She has resolved that she will not return to Allerton Towers a free and fetterless thing. As the Bishop's daughter she knows that she is pretty nearly played out. But as the ambitious, gracious, patronising, powerful wife of a rising man, she may still play a distinguished part in the secular element of clerical life in the diocese.

And who so fitted to rise as the man standing by her side? Her father's chaplain, the one who steers the Bishop over stormy seas with such safety and discretion. There hangs about him, too, a halo of romance, for he has loved her long and well, she firmly believes, and nothing less than the prospect of a coronet would have made her waver from him. As it is, she congratulates herself on the wavering having all been done cautiously and decently, on having been all done " inwardly," in fact, and so being invisible to the naked eye.

In the course of the few minutes that elapse between the ferry-boat leaving the Weybridge bank and gaining the Shepperton side, Miss Templeton, though she watches it with all she has of heart in her eyes, has come to the conclusion that " Mr. Grove deserves to be rewarded by her for his touching devotion and fidelity, and that she will reward him." It will be doubly his duty after this to preserve papa from all those perils to which bishops, who must talk (and can't talk) in convocation and elsewhere, are liable. And it will be doubly pleasant for her to lay this honourable onus upon him now on this evening, when Lord Kenmare may be conceited enough to suppose that she is suffering from his desertion.

It does not occur to her for a moment that, having herself loosened Mr. Grove's shackles, he may be unwilling and unready to tighten them again. He has been so consistently kind, courteous, cheerful, affable, and well satisfied during these last few weeks in which she has been considerately letting him down from the giddy eminence of her flattering regard, that she feels safe in the conviction that he has not observed the change. And though it is mortifying to feel that he has been so unobservant of aught that concerns her, still the law of compensation works, and she admits that in this case it is better so.

It is difficult to begin again with him after being out of practice so long; but mere difficulty is not sufficient to deter Fanny. As soon as she can command her voice, and feel sure of speaking in soft, kindly tones, she replies to his remarks about Ethel making a splendid marchioness and an equally good wife by saying:

" If you *really* think there is a probability of such a happy ending to this thoughtless freak of theirs, they will be just as well pleased to find us gone when they come back as waiting for them."

" Unquestionably they will; are you feeling cold? Shall we go in? " he asks, with amiable, ready, obtuse acquiescence.

" Not in the least cold, and not at all inclined to go in," she says, lowering her voice so that he has to bend his head towards her in order to catch the meaning of her words. Then she turns and abstractedly paces along very slowly in the opposite direction to the homeward one, and, as in duty bound, he courteously paces along by her side.

The moon is making a silver pathway up the river, and the silence around them is unbroken. Now or never is the time for her to indicate to him that she considers their relations to one another are unaltered.

" This is very sweet," she begins, looking up at him, and her face, rising out of the soft masses of a white Shetland shawl, is very young and innocent in the moonlight.

" Very jolly, indeed," he says, heartily. And she replies, " Yet I'm *sure* we both long to get back to the dear old Palace gardens, where we've spent so many, many happy hours together ; this travelling about is very nice, but we always seem to be with other people, and I am getting tired of it ; do let us persuade papa to give up Boyne Gate and go home, when the others leave Weybridge."

" I thought you were enjoying it, and looking forward to the time at Boyne Gate as much as any of us ? " he says, in some surprise ; and then he is conscious that Fanny is appealing to him with all the mute power of appeal there is in woman.

Her eyes are raised with timid tenderness to
his, her hand slips into his arm in order that
she may steady herself in crossing a rugged
bit of turf, and the words she murmurs
tremble on her lips.

"Happy! Yes, I am 'happy,' because
after all, little as we have been seeing of
each other in the old way lately, still we
have been together. But *I* am very faithful
to my love of the old order of things at the
Palace; you never read to me here as you
used to do in the garden at home; these
people come between us and make us seem
to drift apart; and—well! altogether, I shall
be happier when we are home again."

He cannot help understanding that she is
ready to love once again; but he knows that
not only is he not ready, but that he never
will be able to make himself ready any more.
The coldness that he knows has not been
caprice nor uncertainty, but nothing better
than cool calculation on her part, has chilled
and nipped his budding regard for her.
Nothing will ever make it spring forth and
bloom again. But he is a gentleman and he

likes her, and is sorry both for the mistake
she has made in leaving him, and for the
mistake she is now making in coming back
to him.

"You're very fond of the old Palace, are
you not?" he says, kindly; and then he goes
on, "I don't wonder at it either, for I'm
sure if it had been my home as long as it
has been yours, I should be fond of it too."

"Are you not fond of it as it is?" she
asks, with tender reproach, and he thinks
it better for them both that he should be
very matter-of-fact about it.

"I think the Palace a very jolly place to
tent in for a time, but, to tell the truth, I
fear a cathedral-town sphere of work is not
a congenial one to me; it's stagnating; the
chaplaincy is too much of a sinecure for a
strong young fellow like me; I ought to be
in the heat of the battle, and some poor
fellow, who has nearly worn himself out in
his work, ought to have my easy berth."

"Do you mean—you *can't* mean that you
think of leaving?" she gasps.

"Indeed I do, Miss Templeton; I can stand

contact with the rough edges of life, and many of my brethren are physically unable to do that, who yet would fill my present comfortable niche quite as well as I do."

" It will break papa's heart if you leave," she says, vehemently; and then with a sob, she adds in a whisper, "and mine, too."

" I'm sure the Bishop will feel I'm right," Mr. Grove says, discreetly ignoring the whisper. " Look ! they're crossing over again. Shall we go back and meet them ? "

Fanny's clasp on his arm grows tighter. Shall she, the Bishop's daughter, meekly submit to being conquered and discomfited by her father's chaplain. It is not love, but a wild craving desire to carry her point which prompts her now.

" Stop ! " she says, passionately ; " forgive me. I know you have fancied me cold, or not observant of your affection for me, but your threat to go has shown me the state of my own heart. I cannot let you go without telling you that you have entirely won me now—for I cannot part with you."

CHAPTER VIII.

PERHAPS the Bishop's daughter would not pursue her own course with such remorseless zeal were she endowed with the useful gift of prescience, which would enable her to see the way in which her father is improving the shining hour of her absence.

All the romance of the party has not gone out into the moonlight by the river with the young people; in fact, Mrs. Heatherley, whose grace and tact, and happy art of making the best and most of any situation in which she may find herself, has passed into a proverb in her circle, has given the Bishop a glimpse of a blissful domestic picture! And the Bishop has regarded it with affectionately approving eyes.

Practically the mature pair are as much alone as either of the young couples down by

K 2

the river. For Lady St. Just sleeps well after a generous dinner, taken at the close of a long open-air day; and under cover of her reassuringly deep and slumberous breathing, Mrs. Heatherley shows the Bishop how easy a thing it is to cross the delicate neutral line between friendship and love.

"We may not either of us look forward to keeping our dear girls with us much longer," she murmurs, as, from the window which is farthest from Lady St. Just, the Bishop and herself watch the four young people turn the corner to the river.

"And we must prepare to part with them cheerfully, if it is for their happiness that they should go," the Bishop says, heartily. To do him justice he has been quite ready to part with his Fanny any day during the last ten years. At some periods, when her yoke is heavy, it occurs to him to feel that the time is long in getting ripe for her flight from the paternal roof.

"Ah! yes! our love for them will make us seem cheerfully resigned," the fair, bright little widow says, with a mixture of sparkle

and pathos, that calls his attention to the
sweet blue of her eyes, and the exquisite
tenderness of her heart at the same moment;
" but we shall both be very dull and desolate
in our respective homes. When Fanny goes,
and I'm sure it will not be Mr. Grove's fault
if she does not go soon, yours will be a very
solitary life, though you will live it in a
Palace, my friend!"

" Do you think that Grove thinks of this
still? At one time I fancied that affection
was springing up between them, but lately I
have thought there was a certain stiffness and
want of cordiality towards him on Fanny's
part."

Mrs Heatherley's eyes sparkle more than
ever, as she reflects, that the real cause of
the change in Fanny has been the latter's
presumptuous desire to dispute the " big
game"—Lord Kenmare—with Ethel. But
she merely says—

" Trust me for reading these riddles aright.
I am *almost* as sure that your daughter
will be Mrs. Grove as I am that mine will
be Lady Kenmare."

The Bishop pricks up his ears. Good man as he is, he is alive to the value of a good worldly connection, and if Mrs. Heatherley is to be the mother of Lady Kenmare, and by-and-bye, of the Marchioness of Monkstown, who so well fitted as the attractive little widow to be the Bishop's wife, and the enlivener of his solitude.

"I shall give Fanny to Grove with great satisfaction; he will rise on his own merits, for, quite independently of his having any family claim upon me, I shall feel it my duty to give him good preferment; but as you say I shall be a very solitary man when I lose my daughter, and you——!"

He pauses, and his silence is so eloquent that Mrs. Heatherley turns her face coyly away as she replies—

"I suppose rigid Mrs. Grundy will denounce me if I venture to go to the Palace to talk over these *happy* days that we are spending together! Days that unfortunately are only too short, and too nearly at an end."

"Mrs Grundy will never dare to asperse you while I live, dear lady."

"Ah! my dear lord, you forget that I am not so *very* old a woman that you, an attractive man, may dare to be kind to me without calling forth comment—and malignity: yet though I shall be too cowardly ever to *do* it, I will dare to paint a picture of cosy hours spent with you in that grand library—of sunny hours in your lovely grounds—of long delightful readings. I take such a deep, unceasing interest in politics, that when you have the gout I *must* come and read the debates to you——"

"I will not have you contemplate that contingency only," the Bishop says, feeling almost young and *debonair*, as Mrs. Heatherley's facile mental brush puts in the lights and shades of these pleasantly-pictured possibilities. But, though he says this, a vision of himself prostrate and in pain, without the presence of this most soothing woman, rises before him and pleads for her!

She has precisely the voice for reading aloud—clear, sweet, and not too rapid. She is well off, too, and will not limit the hospitalities of the Palace severely, as his

daughter has done at times. If he must
lose Fanny for Fanny's good, who can
blame him for seeking the constant com-
panionship of a mind and heart-stirring
woman, in the most unexceptionable way?
It is not good for bishops to live alone,
more than any other man! She will be
essentially the right woman in the right
place—averse to frivolous gaiety, and admirably contented with cosy hours with
him in the library, and political readings
by his couch of pain.

"I will not have you contemplate the
contingency of my illness only; with you
by my side, constantly, I should be happier
and, therefore, healthier probably, than I
have been since the death of my—I mean
since I have lived a sedentary and secluded
life. The responsibilities of the position I
venture to offer you are many," the Bishop
goes on, with unconscious pomposity. "Its
worldly gaieties are of necessity few; but
your place will be a high one; a fierce
light will shine upon you, and I feel sure
you will bear it bravely."

He pauses, his eloquence checked by an untimely remembrance of his daughter, and of the wrath that young lady will feel and display when she hears of what he has been about in her absence. But Mrs. Heatherley fills the pause graciously.

"I won't affect to misunderstand you," she says, with an amount of womanly self-possession and frankness that is rather embarrassing to him for a moment, for Lady St. Just is giving signs of waking, and he feels that this vital matter is to be clinched in her presence.

"I won't affect to misunderstand you, my lord, and I accept the honour you have done me with the more readiness, because I feel that I shall fill the position of your wife in a way that will redound to *your* credit, as it shall redound to my own."

"She strikes the key-note of the tune to which she means to set our altered lives in that speech," the Bishop says to himself, in a little spasm of alarm at the boldness and irretrievability of the step he has taken. And he is right; Mrs. Heatherley has taken

the reins into her own fair, firm little
hands, and will drive the episcopal chariot
where and how she pleases from this day
forth.

The matter is all settled, and he is receiving
Lady St. Just's congratulations before he has
quite decided in his own mind whether or not
he has asked this woman to be his wife!
Then, in a few minutes, his daughter and his
chaplain come in, and he is observing with
alarm that Fanny's brow is ominously
clouded, and her lips pressed alarmingly
together. Mrs. Heatherley burns his boats
behind him by saying, playfully—

" Tell my new daughter that I am going
to try and fill the place she has adorned so
long, and to share her care of *you*."

To which Miss Templeton replies, unpro-
pitiously, " Papa will never waste his time
in trying to make me believe such an
utterly incredible thing, Mrs. Heatherley."
At which display of temper the pretty widow,
who has won the game, and who can,
therefore, afford to be affable and forgiving, smiles her sunniest smile, and putting

her gentle powerful little paw on her already-tamed Bishop, says:

"I hope, dear, that *my* child will accord you a warmer welcome into her family than your daughter accords me into yours. If you can't give me a daughter's affection, Fanny, I hope at least you will give me a sister's sympathy," she continues, so sweetly, that Fanny feels it will be impolitic to exhibit resentment at the allusion to her having passed girlhood.

"Papa's wife will not stand in need of sympathy from me," she says, brusquely, and Mrs. Heatherley passes by the observation with magnanimous unconcern, feeling sure that she is not the only bitter drop in Fanny's cup at present.

"Allow me to offer you my heartiest congratulations and warmest hopes for your happiness," Mr. Grove says, with a bold acceptance of the situation that enables the Bishop to hold up his head.

Mrs. Heatherley rewards the speaker at once.

"And allow me to say that I hope you will

be very, very often at the Palace to witness that happiness, Mr. Grove, when you can spare the time from the prettiest rectory and parish in the Bishop's gift——"

"Livings are in *papa's* gift, not yours *yet*," Miss Templeton interrupts.

"But he shall not stray about among the vacant ones in solitude and uncertainty as to whom he shall bestow them on any longer," Mrs. Heatherley says, caressingly. "I mean to take the greatest interest in everything you do and think of doing, dear," she continues, and the Bishop smiles feebly, but withal sullenly. To be called " dear," and openly comforted, was not in the agreement he made with himself about the terms he would make with Mrs. Heatherley. However, he keeps silence, for to protest or rebuke, and fail to subdue, would be fatal, indeed, just now.

"I'm afraid I shall *not* be in the way of benefiting by your patronage," Mr. Grove says, blithely and frankly. He is not displeased with Mrs. Heatherley for the tone she has taken—he will be out of the diocese soon; this, for one thing, and, for another, her rule is, or will be, a more graceful one than Fanny's has been. Nevertheless, he is sorry for Fanny, and, if it were possible, he would go back to his old ground with her, and remove her from the humiliations to come.

But it is not possible! He had never been " in love" with her, and now he was quite out of the habit of her; and this he had given her to understand fully and clearly during the last ten minutes which they spent alone together in walking up from the river.

But he had done this with courtesy and consideration; allowing her to suppose that the change in him had been wrought by herself, sparing her all the mortification that is possible, by his manner of suggesting that he has believed it to be her desire to alienate him.

Thus, on the surface, her pride is spared, though in her heart she knows well that his regard for her could never have been as strong as she thought it, since it has been so easily killed.

Nevertheless, this tone, which he has chivalrously taken, will make the task which is before her—of accounting for its being all over between them—a far easier one than it would have been had Mr. Grove simply backed out of the semi-entanglement without this flattering explanation.

Fanny has a keen recollection of having given all and sundry of her lady friends and acquaintances to understand that it rests with herself to convert the bachelor chaplain into the Bishop's son-in-law, any day she pleases. She has even gone so far, in moments of elation, as to hint that his pertinacity and jealousy have been the winning powers that have moved her, and to imply that he had to fight hard and humbly for the victory which he has finally attained over her virgin heart. She knows well that these hints and suggestions will be remembered against her when Mr. Grove openly resigns her and the chaplaincy, and goes off without any visible mark of having suffered in the conflict, upon him. There will be many to say that she has deluded herself all along, and that the love-passages which she has prettily confessed, have been purely imaginary.

By-and-bye Ethel and Lord Kenmare come in, and Mrs. Heatherley is disappointed at the first glance. Kenmare looks dispirited, and Ethel is flushed and distressed in appearance. The girl's first words, too, prove that golden as the opportunity by the moonlighted river has been, the young people have not made the most of it, as Nature and Providence seemed to design, by getting engaged.

"Mother, I want to go home to-morrow instead of going to Boyne Gate; no, Lady St. Just, don't say that I'm tired of you, and don't be angry with me; I can't be happy until I know why Walter Gifford seems to have forgotten me."

"You're not weak enough to waste a thought about a man who even *seems* to have forgotten you, I hope," her mother says, coldly, and the flush deepens on Ethel's brilliant face as she answers:

"Yes, I am; for I know it's only seeming."

"Mr. Gifford must be unlike any other

fellow in the world if he could forget
Miss Heatherley," Lord Kenmare says, with a
gallant effort, "though I wish, with all my
heart, you could forget him," he adds, in a
low tone, to Ethel.

"Perhaps I wish it, too," she murmurs, for
the pertinacious young lover who is present
does contrast favourably just now with the
apparently negligent one who is absent. And
on the strength of these words, uttered partly
in pique and partly in idleness, Lord Kenmare
determines to persist in his suit, and to finally
win both Ethel and his father to regard it
favourably.

"I want to speak to you in my room to-
night, Ethel," Mrs. Heatherley says, rising up
and silently extending her hand to the Bishop,
who takes it and retains it long enough to
give Ethel time to see that something has happened between her mother and the Bishop.
Then the newly-betrothed pair separate, and
the Bishop says good-night to Ethel in a paternal and benedictory way that informs her of
the truth, before her mother can word it
touchingly and gracefully.

"Mother," the girl begins, as soon as she gets into her mother's room, "what is it? what does it mean? The Bishop patted my head as if I had been a little child, and Fanny glared at me as if I had wanted him to do it—what does it mean?"

"Before I tell you that, tell me *what* you mean by making a scene about Mr. Gifford," Mrs. Heatherley says, reproachfully.

Ethel's arms are round her mother's neck in a moment. The girl wants to be strengthened and supported in her intention of being leal to her absent lover. She is made of the stuff to hate herself if she does eventually fall away from her freely given promise to marry Walter Gifford by-and-bye. Yet, all the while she feels that Lord Kenmare, with his warmly-proffered love, his great personal beauty, and his winning way, is a great temptation to her.

"Oh, mother! say something kind of Walter; help me to keep on loving him best," she pleads, with her arms clinging closely round her mother's neck.

"My dear Ethel, nonsense! Mr. Gifford

is showing plainly that he can resign you,
and it is your duty to me and to yourself
to regard your engagement with him as at
an end. I am not going to say anything
to you about Lord Kenmare more than
this: that his preference for you demands
this return—that you do nothing hastily;
it would grieve the Bishop—to say nothing
of myself—if you raise any objection to
going to Boyne Gate.

"The Bishop has nothing to do with me,
and if I do what I think right I don't
care whether he's grieved or not."

"The Bishop's wishes are paramount with
me; in running counter to his desire for
your welfare, you will be directly opposing
me—your mother!"

"Oh, Mother! *don't* bring him in between
us," Ethel says, tempestuously. "What can
it be to him whether I go to Boyne Gate,
or, for the matter of that, whether I ever
speak to Lord Kenmare again?"

"The Bishop does me honour in proposing
to become my husband, and he does *you*
honour, Ethel, in proposing to treat you as

his own daughter," Mrs. Heatherley says,
with the air of patient sweetness that she
has invariably found useful in the subjuga-
tion of Ethel.

"Mother, dear, let him do you all the
honour he can—he can't show you too much
homage for your goodness in giving your
darling, pretty self to his service; but don't
let him try to 'befather' me; if he wants
Lord Kenmare in the family for his own
honour and glory's sake, let him marry
Kenmare to Fanny."

"You were never a silly child, Ethel,
always my brightest and best companion;
don't be a silly girl!" and with these words
Mrs. Heatherley dismisses her daughter with
a kiss, and proceeds to write an autumn
programme for herself.

"Let me see!" she says, meditatively
pausing, pen in hand, for a minute or two;
"a fortnight at Boyne Gate will bring us
to the middle of September; by that time
Ethel will be settled—the child is too
sensible to continue contumacious, and
Kenmare is too fascinating to be resisted

long. Then home for a month of preparation! The weddings shall be the third week in October, and before I sleep I'll write to Worth about the dresses."

CHAPTER IX.

"ALL the place is talking about it, so it must be true," Miss Gifford says, angrily and conclusively, to her brother, when he disputes her assertion that there is to be a double wedding at the cottage soon, when Mrs. Heatherley will take the Bishop to honour and obey her, and her daughter will marry Lord Kenmare.

"Lily and I have been in at Turner's," Miss Gifford continues, animatedly, "and they showed us the order for the costumes, eight for Mrs. Heatherley, and eight for Miss Heatherley. The bridal dresses are coming from Paris, Mrs. Turner says, but there is no doubt about these eight a-piece being *trousseau* dresses, and so, naturally, there is no doubt about Miss Heatherley going to marry Lord Kenmare."

"I will not believe it yet," Mr. Gifford

says, stoutly; but it vexes him to see that his sister and her friend exchange smiles that seem fraught with pity for his contemptible blindness.

"I would not believe it—yet," Lily Somerset says, quietly. "I would wait on in patient endurance until the wedding-day, and all doubt is over, if I were a man and in your place. I would give the woman I loved all the satisfaction and honour and glory I could. I would not give her indifference for indifference, scorn for scorn; I would show her that I was the real 'gentle tassel,' ready to be whistled back again at any moment. But when I had done all this, and been re-quited by her according to my deserts, I would never dare to ask another woman to love me."

Walter Gifford strokes his moustache, meditatively, as he listens to this harangue, which Miss Somerset delivers with the most absolute composure, in silvery, unruffled accents.

"I am never likely to ask another woman to love me," he says, presently, and Lily

nods her head at him in an approving way
that provokes rather than soothes him.

"Of course, you are not likely to do it;
it will be only due to Lady Kenmare to show
her that where she has ruthlessly wounded
no other can heal. And what an amusing
story Mrs. Templeton will make out of your
fidelity to her beautiful daughter; you'll be
the topic at the Bishop's dinners and the
Bishopess's garden-parties for a time; and I
shouldn't wonder if the fact of your wearing
the willow publicly increased your practice
considerably. I hope it will, I am sure, for
the law of compensation ought to work in
some way."

"It is working already," he says, trying
to speak gaily; "it is making you think
about me, and talk to me more than you
have for years."

They are sitting in the rafter-roofed, old-
world sitting-room at the Uplands; it is easy
for Miss Gifford to slip out of the room at
this juncture without distracting their attention, or in any way disturbing them. The
daylight is waning, and the moon has not

risen yet. From their seats in the wide
window-recess, the old-fashioned garden, in
which pear and apple trees are mixed up in
picturesque confusion with tall hollyhocks
and sun-flowers, and feathery plants of
waving asparagus that has gone luxuriantly
to seed, looks quaint and attractive. Just
under the window a mass of lemon-thyme
and mint surrounds a few sweet-scented
bushes of late-flowering roses. Altogether
there is a softening, subduing influence in the
beauty and the perfume that permeates the
atmosphere. And Walter Gifford, wearied
as he is by a hard day's work, and many
conflicting emotions about his absent Ethel,
feels that it is pleasant to look upon so fair
a scene with such a sympathetic companion.

Pleasant but dangerous, as Lily droops
the face that is as fair as her name with
languid tenderness towards him, and murmurs
in reply—

"Does it please you that I should *show* the
interest I have never ceased to feel in you by
saying bitter things of the girl who has won
your love only to throw it away like an old

glove? Oh! I am vexed with myself for having been so weak as to give you such an occasion for triumphing over me."

"Heaven knows I have never felt triumphant where you have been concerned," he says, moodily; "and even now I know that you only portray interest in me as you gather flowers—to please yourself for the moment."

"Walter, you wrong me, indeed you do, in thinking so of me now; there was a time when I did not appreciate you, a time when in my egotism I told you so for granted that I did not think it possible to wear out your regard by my caprices; but you taught me a sharp lesson, and I have learnt it well; you can't forgive, any more than I can forget."

"I forgave you all the pain you made me suffer long ago," he says, frankly; "but you are right in hinting that I can't reconstruct the old romance; you wouldn't be happy if I attempted to do it; you would feel naturally that you deserved more than grateful friendship, which is all that I can ever offer you."

"——If Ethel Heatherley had never existed you would be more forgiving to me!"

"You shall not speak of forgiveness; you broke the chain of feeling which once bound us together, yourself; I haven't the power of re-uniting the links, that is all. Perhaps if Ethel Heatherley had never existed I should have carried *my* end of the chain up to this present day; as it is——"

"She will cease to exist for you when she becomes Lady Kenmare?"

"She will—God bless her! but she is not Lady Kenmare yet, nor will she ever be," he says, heartily, gathering fresh faith in Ethel from the force of his own words.

Lily leans through the open window and gathers a sprig of something at random. It happens to be mint, and as she presses it and smells it, and then hands it to him, she says, prosaically, and as if the preceding conversation had not been one of vital interest to her, "We shall always think of each other and of what we have been saying in future when we see roast lamb and mint sauce, shan't we? shockingly commonplace, isn't it? but so *true*, and we both like truth."

Then she rises from the window, and goes

back to a corner in the room where an old piano stands, and, sitting down to it, she begins to sing " In the Gloaming."

As her soul-fraught voice gives power and pathos to the song. which in itself is mere prettiness, Mr. Gifford, who has borne himself bravely in the battle up to this point, feels that he is vulnerable after all. Why, if Ethel is false, should "what has been" with Lily "never be again?"

" To love is best, but to be loved is good," he tells himself, and there is something of this sentiment expressed in the way he holds Lily Somerset's hand when he says goodnight to her.

"Well!" Mabel, the over-anxious sister, asks eagerly, as she comes back to the room after accompanying her brother to the garden gate, " Well, how are you and Walter getting on?"

" We shall get on better when Miss Heatherley is married."

" It's *tame* of Walter to wait till all the world has seen that she has thrown him over," Miss Gifford says, indignantly, and forthwith she determines to do something rather desperate, for the sake of what she deems the honour, and dignity, and happiness of her brother.

Miss Gifford does not hold the pen of a ready writer, therefore her self-appointed task is a laborious one, and occupies her well-nigh through all the hours of the night. Weariness and sleepiness is her portion in the morning, but she gets up bravely and waits upon Lily Somerset as assiduously as ever, for she has upon her the pleasing consciousness of having done a good work for her brother.

This " good work " goes forth by the midday post from Allerton Towers in the guise of a letter to Miss Heatherley, whose address the devoted sister has procured, at the cost of a considerable amount of speciously worded enquiry, from the head milliner at Turner's shop, and Ethel receives it three or four days after her arrival at Boyne Gate.

It is as follows :—

" DEAR MADAM,—

        " I must begin by offering you a profound apology for the liberty which I, a

stranger, take in addressing you at all.
Nothing but the earnest desire I have to see
the welfare and happiness of my dear brother
secured could excuse this conduct, even in
my own eyes.

"A rumour has reached us that you are
about to make a brilliant marriage very
shortly, but my brother refuses to accept the
release from his engagement to you until he
hears from you that he may take his freedom
honourably. My reason for hoping that you
will act thus generously is, that I have good
reason to know that my brother would find
happiness with another, if it were not for his
scruples concerning you; and I am sure,
from what I have heard of your nobility of
character, you would not wish to stand in
his way now that you have preferred another
to him.

"My brother is not aware of my intention
of writing to you, nor do I wish him to
know it, as, unless he feels that your action
is spontaneous, and not the result of inter-
ference, he may refuse to be influenced by it.

"In conclusion, my dear young lady, let

me pray you again to pardon this bold act
of mine, and to believe that I am actuated
solely by my affection for my brother, and
my heartfelt belief that what I ask you to
do will enable him to become a happy and
wealthy man.

"I am, dear Madam,

"Respectfully yours,

"MABEL GIFFORD."

Happily for herself, Ethel is alone when
she receives this extraordinary epistle. Her
first indignant impulse upon reading it, is
to enclose it to Walter, without a word. Her
next is to write to him, asking, "if it can be
true that he is not only willing to let her go,
but ready to console himself with 'another,'
as his sister puts it?" This is the reasonable
and right impulse! Unfortunately, however,
Ethel does not act upon it, but reads the
letter over again and again, until her whole
soul is filled with anger and mortification, and
while this last and worst mood is upon her
she writes to Walter—

"Do not let any further thought of me
weigh with you for a moment longer. I

have gone out of your life for ever! and I can only hope that you will seek happiness where you can find it, and as soon as possible forget that Ethel Heatherley ever existed."

"Mother," she says, an hour or two afterwards, coming upon that lady and the Bishop in one of the many sequestered walks that intersect the Boyne Gate grounds, "I have something to tell you."

The girl turns into a side path, and looks as if she expected her mother to follow her. But Mrs. Heatherley is indisposed to do anything that may look like independent action in the eyes of the Bishop.

"You may feel sure that the Bishop will listen with glad interest to anything that concerns you, dear," she says, with her freshest, youngest air of innocent reliance on the Bishop's affections; but Ethel is in the wrong mood to return her mother's fascinating lead.

"If you won't come and hear my news, mother, I will keep it for a more convenient season," the disappointed daughter says, with a catch in her voice that appeals to so much as is motherly in the vain little widow's heart.

"Spare me for a few moments, will you?" she says, coquettishly; "my child is a little tiny bit jealous of the time I give to you, I'm afraid;" then she adds in a whisper, "she reveres you too much to speak familiarly before you *yet*, but love will soon cast out fear when you are her father."

"Very proper, nice feeling on her part, I am sure," the Bishop says, benignly. To tell the. truth, reverence is not precisely the sentiment with which he himself fancies he has inspired his pretty widow's handsome daughter. Nor, indeed, to do him justice, does he desire to insist upon a display of filial feeling from the young lady. But, for the future, his ways and wishes will be moulded and guided by a stronger hand than his own, and, like a man, he prepares to bow to the inevitable.

So Mrs. Heatherley trips along after Ethel, who walks rapidly to a recess in the high laurel hedge, where she stops, and begins at once—

" I have broken off my engagement with Walter Gifford to-day, mother; don't ask me why I have done it, and don't build any fallacious hopes upon it. I have done it! and I'm more unhappy than I ever thought it possible I could be; but I don't want to go back to Allerton Towers. I would rather go away where no one will ever speculate about me and my lost happiness."

" My darling, you will be rewarded for this obedience to my wishes, and to the dictates of common sense, by meeting with one who will make your lot a far happier one than it could ever have been as Mr. Gifford's wife," Mrs. Heatherley says, rapturously; but Ethel shakes her head and says—

" No, mother, you will be burdened with me all my life, or rather the Bishop will be; I won't let myself fancy anything so evil as that *you* will ever wish me away from you."

Again the maternal instinct is aroused, and tears of genuine feeling for her daughter well up into Mrs. Heatherley's bright blue eyes. · But when she speaks there is a nervous quiver in her voice that sounds more like fear than love.

"I shall never know a moment's peace, Ethel, my darling, till you are well married, and removed from the possibility of any change in my fortunes affecting you."

Ethel smiles sadly.

"My dear little mother, for your sake the Bishop won't grudge me a corner in the Palace, and, if he does, why shouldn't I live on at the cottage?"

"There are many reasons why; but it's ridiculous to talk seriously in this strain," Mrs. Heatherley says, sharply; and for a few moments she looks quite middle-aged and haggard. Then with an effort she resumes her youth and gaiety, and runs back to the Bishop as if her feet were not shackled, and her brow burdened with a weight of secret care.

"I must tell you the good news at once; my dear child has made me *quite* happy by freeing herself from that foolish entanglement with the young surgeon," she says, sliding her hand under the Bishop's arm.

" It was not a *regular* engagement, I understand ? " he asks, and she tells him—

" Oh, no ! a foolish arrangement between two thoughtless young people, of which I never could approve ; his connections are not in our class of life at all, I should say, from the little I saw of his sister."

" I can never bring myself to countenance a breach of such a solemn thing as a regular, authorised, sensible engagement," his lordship says, sternly. Then, having asserted his prerogative to judge and condemn, he relapses into affability, and expresses a hope that Lord Kenmare will now catch Ethel's heart in the rebound.

"I shall certainly advise him to seize this golden opportunity," he says ; and Mrs. Heatherley, who dreads the effect of anything like interference on his part, is obliged to entreat him to observe the golden rule of silence when Ethel's heart affairs are concerned.

" In good time it will all arrange itself,

I am sure," she says, confidently, for she does not dare to allow herself to doubt and fear about Ethel's future. If her daughter does not make a wealthy marriage, with a man who will for love of Ethel be both liberal and discreet, the blithe little widow, who has always passed for a wealthy one in Allerton Towers society, will be poor indeed.

Lord Kenmare has not accompanied them to Boyne Gate. A letter from his father, peremptorily demanding his son's immediate presence at Sir John Hawtrey's house hard by, has relieved Ethel from the embarrassing daily intercourse with the young man whom she has refused to marry, but whom she likes with a warmer liking than she has for anyone else on earth, excepting Walter Gifford!

She must not be thought either inconsistent or fickle, when it is said of her that there has been so much sweetness in this daily intercourse that she misses it very sadly now that it is over. There are moments when she longs for his presence again, longs to hear his ardent adoring words, that will not be silenced; longs to see his boyishly frank displayal of desperate regard for her; longs, in fact, for the sight of "the only one who is true and loyal and staunch to her," as she tells herself, thinking sorrowfully of Walter.

It must be admitted that life is not very lively at Boyne Gate. Lady St. Just having failed in bringing matters to a successful issue between Lord Kenmare and Ethel, and being rather annoyed than otherwise at her old friend, the Bishop, having suffered himself to fall captive to Mrs. Heatherley's bow and spear, is rather tired of this family party which she has brought upon herself. If Ethel would only be sensible, and accept the love that is offered to her, Lady St. Just would take the credit of making the match to herself next season, and feel pride and pleasure. But as Ethel is contumacious, there is a flatness about the group, which falls upon Lady St. Just, who revenges herself by being so depressing that even the Bishop feels that the atmosphere of his Palace is exhilarating by comparison.

"I can't help thinking that our friend is expecting a fresh relay of guests; possibly it may not suit her arrangements to have us here any longer," he hints to his bride-elect. But she, having her own reasons for staying away from Allerton Towers until her wedding-day is near at hand, tells him that "for her child's sake she has resolved to stay and meet and conquer Lord Monkstown."

It is a little thing to Mrs. Heatherley, who has large things at stake, that her august hostess should be obviously tired of her and her future spouse.

"He *is* heavy, deadly heavy, when he emerges from the cloudy splendour of bishop-hood, and becomes a mere man, affecting harmless sprightliness," Mrs. Heatherley says to herself, with a laugh and a shrug of the pretty supple shoulders—whose undulations the Bishop is observing at the moment with admiring eyes—"but I shall have to endure the burden of being bored by him so long as we both do live. Why shouldn't Lady St. Just have a sensation of what I shall have to bear? Ethel and I compensate her amply for

Fanny's cautious insipidity, and her father's excellent uninterestingness." So for the sake of a certain something, which she does not confide either to her child Ethel, or her captive Bishop, Mrs. Heatherley puts her pride aside, and stays on where she is obviously not wanted.

Success appears about to crown her in one direction, at least, when she hears that on the following day " six guns," chosen for their well-known prowess over turnip fields and against partridges, are going out from Boyne Gate for a hard day's work, and that their arduous labours are to be relieved by the ladies and luncheon at Bale Coppice at half-past one. For among these six are the Marquis of Monkstown and his son, Lord Kenmare.

"I hear that Lord Monkstown is a sweet old man," Mrs. Heatherley says to the Bishop; "and I am sure when he sees Ethel, and finds how perfectly she behaves, never giving Kenmare the slightest encouragement to make love to her, and yet showing her liking for him in such a pretty, frank way,

I am sure, quite, quite sure that he will support his son's suit, and that our darling Ethel will be made happy almost against her will."

"A Higher Power than ours directs these things," the Bishop says, with the impressive tone that is pronounced to be "very telling" by his admirers when he is giving a Charge full of flawless commonplaces. But at the same time, despite this verbal expression of pious reliance, he is glad that Mrs. Heatherley will have such an excellent opportunity of lending a mundane hand towards the formation of so gratifying a connection.

There is a sort of tacit agreement between Lady St. Just and Mrs. Heatherley to the effect that Ethel shall not be told that Lord Kenmare and his father will meet them at Bale Coppice this day. Accordingly, Ethel allows herself to be bent and moulded to their wishes and wills without a murmur. There is a good deal of the managing faculty required in order to transport the house party to the trysting-place comfortably and consistently. It is clear to the most opaque secular mind that the gaiters and hat of a bishop must not be shown to the eye of dissent (which prevails in these parts) descending from a little Norfolk cart. Therefore Mrs. Heatherley is compelled to accompany the wearer of these honourable but oppressive insignia in the landau with Lady St. Just, instead of going, as her taste would dictate, in the Norfolk cart drawn by the sporting-looking little cob which is driven by Ethel.

And to make matters worse, it seems, fate decrees that, for the greater convenience of the greater number. Fanny Templeton shall be Ethel's companion. Fanny Templeton, who will squeeze herself into every little crevice of an opportunity which judicious management may make for Kenmare to have uninterrupted intercourse with Ethel. Mrs. Heatherley's brow darkens and her eyes glare at her future step-daughter, as Fanny takes her place—and Fanny's intuition tells her the reason why.

"Your mamma is afraid I shall be in your way, dear," she says, at once, and Ethel, taking her literally, replies—

"Oh! nonsense; there's plenty of room—room for one behind as far as that goes; Mr. Grove, why don't you come with us?" she cries out, as the chaplain is preparing to step into the landau, and without hesitation Mr. Grove turns and accepts the invitation.

For a few minutes Fanny is silenced by this move on the board, but as they dash out into the lane which leads to Bale Coppice she recovers her wonted equanimity, and power of uttering that which is most likely to discompose her audience.

"I am feeling quite anxious to see Lord Monkstown, are not you, Ethel? They say he's such a fascinating, courtly old gentleman, and as handsome, even now, as Lord Kenmare."

The cob bends his nose in half an inch more, and steps out a thought quicker, thus indicating that he has felt a sudden pressure on his bit. This is the only sign given that the name so lightly mentioned has gone home to the heart of the hearer.

"Is Lord Monkstown one of the party?"

Ethel asks, holding her face well round for Miss Templeton's inspection.

"Why; yes, of course, you know that both he and Kenmare are here," Fanny rejoins, and at the same moment the cob swerves sharply round a corner close to the coppice.

CHAPTER X.

THE cob has distanced his more majestic stable brethren in the landau, and the consequence is, Ethel finds herself dashing up to the group of six expectant, hungry men, with the air of being so eager to join them that she has outstripped conventionality, and left her *chaperone* behind her.

The clear, bright, dark face lights up radiantly, and the soft, dark velvet eyes are lustrous with a variety of deeply-stirred feelings, as, foremost among the group of men, the girl recognises Lord Kenmare. She cannot help feeling pleased at the warm pleasure with which he comes to greet her. She cannot help feeling flattered at the flattering heart-and-lip-homage he renders her. She cannot help being proud of the pride he takes in showing all those who care to

sec it, that his devotion to Ethel Heatherley
is unaltered.

He is by the side of the Norfolk cart the
moment the cob stops, doffing his hat low
to the young lady, whose pretty blushes
might pass for the red flag of love in the
eyes of one less keen to detect the truth
than he is.

"May I introduce my father to you?" he
asks, and presently Ethel feels her hand taken
very kindly by a handsome old gentleman,
who is merely a splendidly-matured edition
of Kenmare.

"*This* is the obstacle to my wishes with
regard to Caroline," Lord Monkstown thinks,
and he resolves to ignore Kenmare's infatua-
tion altogether, since the latter has never
confided the name of the object of it to the
paternal ear.

"The boy wears his heart upon his sleeve,"
the father says to himself, as Ethel springs
out of the trap, and Kenmare at once en-
deavours to draw her away from the others
"to look at a view of Boyne Gate from the
other end of the coppice." But Lord Monks-

town does not think this angrily, by any
means. He is not displeased that his son's
first serious heart-affection should have been
given him by a girl who would so gracefully
wear the title and coronet of a marchioness
as Ethel. " It must never be with Kenmare,
but she amply justifies the boy's admiration
for her, and desire to have her," the old
nobleman—who prides himself upon estimat-
ing women correctly, and specially plumes
himself on the aptitude of his power of dis-
cerning whether or not they are fitted by
nature and habit to hold high places—thinks.
" It must never be——with Kenmare ; but
if he gets over it, or rather *when* he gets
over it "—Lord Monkstown checks even his
thoughts at this juncture, but they have
run away with him far enough for it to be
nearly a certainty that if Ethel is ambitious
only, her ambition may be gratified by
another than Kenmare !

That something of this is shadowed forth
in the long, admiring gaze which the old
gentleman sends after the supple, erect figure
which is stepping along so lightly in the

distance by the side of his son, may be
gathered from the fact that Fanny Templeton
feels impelled to say as soon as an introduc-
tion enables her to address Lord Monkstown:

"Have you never seen my pretty friend
before?"

"I have never had the pleasure of meeting
Miss Heatherley until to day," he replies.

"Ah! your son has the advantage of you
in that respect at least," Fanny says, putting
on a look of tender regard for the young girl,
whom she would willingly obliterate from the
face of the earth at the present moment, were
such a course feasible without unpleasant
results to herself. Then, as Lord Monkstown
acquiesces in her statement that his own son
has the advantage of him, Fanny goes on—

"Lord Kenmare and Miss Heatherley are
quite old friends, and would have been something more, I have heard, if it had not been
for the prior claims of Mr. Walter Gifford."

"Indeed!"—Lord Monkstown startled a
little, not as Fanny supposes by the suggestion that his son has been in love with Ethel,
but by the idea of any other man being for-

tunate enough to have a prior claim to her—
"indeed! and who is Mr. Walter Gifford?"

"A surgeon in practice in Allerton Towers,
a good sort of young man, I believe, not that
I know anything of him, for, of course, he's
not in our set."

"At the same time you are so intimate
with his *fiancée*."

Lord Monkstown put it in this way, hoping
that he may be told immediately that Ethel
is *not a fiancée*, but the feline Fanny has no
intention of putting the noble mover out
of pain or suspense quickly.

"I am so intimate with his *fiancée*, because
her mother and the Bishop, my father, are
going to be foolish enough to marry one
another in their old age. Then she remembers that Lord Monkstown must be the
Bishop's senior by many a long year, and
adds an amendment:

"Not that my father's age is against the
wisdom of the intention, I don't think that
for a moment; but Mrs. Heatherley is
certainly long past the age at which it might
have been easy to tear her from the habits

to which she is wedded, and mould her to a new manner of life."

"There is nothing that can be said against Mrs. Heatherley's prudence; she has shown it in accepting the Bishop," the Marquis says, smiling, and, as he speaks, the landau with its highly esteemed cargo comes lumbering up respectably, and kind little Fanny is unable to put any more pins into the noble pin-cushion for the time.

As soon as Mrs. Heatherley comes into collision with Lord Monkstown, she understands that she must renounce her intention of creating a paternal regard for Ethel in his heart. He is no "heavy father" to hold out against the projected union of the young people, for whom she is scheming, for a time, and then to endow them with countless thousands and his blessing. He is, on the contrary, a fine, handsome, rather vain; attractive, rather selfish man, who banishes his age as much from his own mind, and from the sight of other people, as possible. A man in whom the pride of life is still strong enough for it to be extremely probable that he will prefer having a beautiful, penniless young wife for himself, to permitting his son to enjoy the luxury.

All this is so patent to Mrs. Heatherley, that she, being in her own eyes a still young and remarkably pretty woman, is almost disposed to regret that the proclamation of her victory over the Bishop has gone forth. Her unfailing instinct for the fitness of things tells her that she would have made a better marchioness than she will a bishop-ess. But as this is not in the alterable order of things, Mrs. Heatherley makes up her mind to succumb to the inevitable, graciously and gracefully.

She still has a trump card in her hand! "Ethel is the most marriageable girl I ever saw in my life, if she can only be induced to marry," she tells herself; and then she looks at the Marquis and makes plans!

"Dear old man!—so distinguished-looking! After all, there's nothing finer on the face of the earth than a real Irish gentleman. And the Marquis of Monkstown may safely chal-lenge criticism. An old man's darling.

What better fortune for a fortuneless girl can be desired? An old man's darling! And that old man a venerable Adonis and a marquis!"

"My daughter is such a perfect child of nature, that she forgets other people may animadvert upon her conduct; she treats Lord Kenmare with the simple familiarity she would show towards a younger brother; forgetting that unkind eyes may see more in her manner than she means, and unkind tongues mention it."

Mrs. Heatherley says this in plaintively apologetic accents to Lord Monkstown, in a brief interval—during which she has him entirely to herself—while the luncheon is being spread. It is not through neglecting the Bishop that this opportunity arises, but rather that he is allowing himself to be absorbed by a communication his daughter has just made to him.

"Papa," Fanny says, as she sees Mrs. Heatherley preparing to melt Lord Monkstown, "I want to show you a fern that we ought to have for our grates, it spreads so beautifully." Then, while the Bishop is looking in blind confidence for the fern, in the direction his daughter indicates, she stabs him ruthlessly:

"Papa, do you know that woman is hopelessly, irretrievably, scandalously in debt?"

"I don't believe—I mean what woman are you speaking about?" he says, wincing pitifully under the pain, but struggling still to preserve an air of composure.

"You know I can only mean Mrs. Heatherley."

"And you know Mrs. Heatherley is to be my wife, Fanny; I can't listen to gossip about her, even from you."

"But the gossip is true, papa; I have heard to-day, on excellent authority, that Mrs. Heatherley is only marrying you because she has wasted her daughter's substance and her own; she is nothing better than an extravagant pauper."

"It would be treason to myself were I to listen to such an evil report," the Bishop says, strengthening himself in his determination to be staunch by the reflection that he is too firmly in Mrs. Heatherley's clutches ever to hope to get out of them.

"It is worse treason to yourself to turn a deaf ear to what I tell you, papa," Fanny persists, and to do her justice, she has good grounds for what she says, and is not actuated by an unkindly spirit towards Mrs. Heatherley only. It is gall and wormwood to her to think of the widow as the presiding genius of the Palace, but there is worse bitterness in the thought that the widow will bring no grist to the mill.

"At any rate, enquire into her affairs before you take the fatal step, papa," she urges, and the Bishop, who has a quiet conviction that he is going to his doom in making this marriage, promises her that he will "be cautious."

"At the same time, understand that I have every confidence—*every* confidence in Mrs. Heatherley," he says, emphatically— so emphatically, in fact, that he almost believes himself. But his daughter knows better, and in the unconvinced toss her head gives there is another dagger-thrust.

Meanwhile Ethel and Lord Kenmare are looking at the view on the sheltered side of Bale Coppice.

"Did you think I should be here to-day?" he asks, when they have rounded a corner and found a bank thickly-cushioned with moss, to sit down upon.

"I didn't think about you before I started."

"But, after you had started, did I come into your head at all? Give me that much pleasure at least—say you thought I should be here, and still you came."

"You were put into my head by Fanny Templeton; she told me just as we drove up to you, that 'of course I knew both your father and you were here! I didn't know, but that was her way of putting it."

"I hope you'll like my father."

"I hope I shall," Ethel says, politely. It does not seem a matter of vital consequence whether she likes his father or not, but, as he wishes it, she does not feel disposed to cavil at the expression of his desire.

"Yes," the young man goes on, I hope

with all my heart you'll like my father, because if you do he'll soon think all the world of you, and the other will be no-where."

"I don't want him to think all the world of me," Ethel says, anxiously; "it would be such a pity, such a waste you know, if he did! And who's the other one?"

"Oh! I forgot you didn't know about my cousin, Caroline Hawtrey; she's the governor's craze; she's an heiress, and she's his niece, and she's destined by both her own father and mine to be Lady Kenmare; and, look here, Ethel, whether you will in time, or not, I don't mean to have it."

"To have what?"

"You know what—Caroline for my wife; she's a good little thing, meek, and gentle, and nice-looking; but, after seeing you, and seeing what I do in you, I cannot see any-thing in her strong enough to blot you out."

"I think most men fall in love two or three times, in a fanciful way, before they meet the women they marry."

" I think I've heard that remark made before," he laughs. " Miss Heatherley, even when you try to be tame and trite you're more interesting than any other girl."

" I have not been sufficiently interesting to Mr. Gifford to keep him true to me," she says, sorrowfully. " Just think; I'm as fond of him as you are of—anybody, and I've had to give him up because he has seen a girl he likes better than me."

" I don't believe it."

" Do you mean you don't believe he's tired of me ? " she asks, eagerly.

" Yes, that's what I do mean ; I wish I could run him down with all my heart; I wish I could dare to say that I think him a hound. But I don't, you see ; if any one has told you that he's tired of you and that he likes someone else better, that someone must have lied, because he *couldn't*, you know !—the thing isn't in man ' to do.' "

" I think you're better than anyone else, you're nobler ; you can't imagine low, false things ; oh ! you are so true, and you are so generous!" Ethel says, vigorously, and, instantly, she wishes she had not said it, for Lord Kenmare takes heart of grace from her encouragement to say:

"You never say a thing you don't mean, I've found that out about you; and so, as you mean you think all these good things of me—can't you, *can't* you love me, dear?"

"I wish I could—I am an unfortunate girl, I think, Lord Kenmare," she says, with a sweet seriousness that appeals to all that is noblest in his noble nature. "At least," she adds, hurriedly, as if she fears she were doing injustice to someone, "I seem to be unfortunate just now, but, perhaps, it's only seeming; the two people I think most of in the world—the two I love the best and *want* to trust the most, 'seem' to be getting away from me."

"And one of these is this Mr. Gifford?" he asks, with kindly curiosity.

"Yes, one of them is 'this Mr. Gifford,' as you choose to call him," Ethel says, perking her head up in proud deprecation of the depreciation which is implied in that word

" only ; " " and that he should fall off, or seem weak and wanting, is a trouble heavy enough to embitter my life, for I thought him higher than myself, you know, and—"

She pauses suddenly, and a light, as of a new revelation, springs up into her face.

" I forgot," she whispers, bending her pretty head, with pretty modesty, " I forgot! the one who has taken him from me may be so much better than me, that it was only right of him to go."

This is a view of the case which Kenmare cannot combat. When Ethel is lowly, she is a beloved but still an overwhelming burden.

" But it can never be made to look right that mother should marry the Bishop," Ethel goes on, looking him direct in the face, in a way that makes him feel that it will be idle on his part to utter a mere platitude. " It will always look a strained and incongruous arrangement—and it will be worse than it looks. And I can't bear it, for I love my mother."

" She is a free agent," Lord Kenmare remarks, suggestively. He is afraid to assert anything, yet he wishes to show that he has a healthy yearning for information on all points that concern Miss Heatherley.

"Yes—mother's a free agent, as far as being well-off and quite independent of every one goes; but mother has a very gentle and reliant nature—oh! she's ever so much more inclined to yield and to lean upon people than I am."

"And the Bishop is a good, massive leaning-post!"

"That's just it; dear mother has lived her graceful, unprotected life long enough for her to have gained reliance on herself; but, somehow or other, she hasn't got it; she's afraid of what people may say of her and of me! as if it mattered! and she fancies when she is the Bishop's wife that we shall both be founded on a rock."

"If I were you I wouldn't fret myself about my mother's marriage. The Bishop's worst fault, as far as I can see, is that he's a deuced nuisance to talk to; and, if your mother can stand that, you needn't worry yourself about it, need you?"

" I often wonder what people go on talking about all through the long years—for ever so long—for so long as they both do live—as, when they're married, and all the furniture is got, and they know who's going to call and who isn't, there can't be much more to say ; " and he replies, with the decision that is an attribute of his age—

"They don't talk to each other, you know."

" Do you mean that husbands and wives don't talk to each other? "

"Not as a rule—but—you and your husband will be an exception ; I could go on talking with you for ever without feeling tired, or thinking that a change would be pleasant."

" Ah ! but you're not my husband," she says, lightly ; " and if you were we should soon wear the topics we have in common, threadbare ; now, with a man who had a profession, it would be different. I should take an interest in his cases, and speak about them——"

" ——Is there any path in life that I can tread that will awake interest enough in you

to make me follow it," he interrupts, eagerly;
"I'll go in for politics with my whole heart
if you'll put a bit of heart into my doing
so."

"If I weighed with you for a moment—
if you thought of me when you went into
the strife, your whole heart wouldn't be in
your work, therefore you'd do it badly."

"May I not hope to touch a noble aim, and
then lay fondly at your feet the fulness of my
fame?" he asks, and then Ethel gives him
a sharp thrust with the sword of commonsense.

"If your father knew the way in which
you are misusing your privileges, how angry
he would be with you and with me; and
don't make him angry with me—I want him
to like me."

"For my sake?" he mutters.

"No, not for your sake at all; but because
he's a grander gentleman than I've ever seen
before, and so I should like him to like me,
and make much of me, for my own sake."

The girl is very much in earnest, and only
a little in jest, in saying this. Nevertheless,

it startles and almost hurts her when he answers, gravely:

"I hope and trust that it may be for your 'own sake,' for your sake will be mine."

Even as he says this, the old Marquis rounds the corner of the coppice, escorted by Mrs. Heatherley and Fanny Templeton. The Bishop would not come "because the wasps worry him," they explain; and Lady St. Just wishes the elaborately-prepared luncheon to be eaten without further delay. But Ethel cannot help feeling that neither the importunity of the wasps assailing, as they do, the current comfort of a Bishop, nor the urgency of the case as regards the luncheon, would have brought Lord Monkstown round the coppice corner in search of her.

"For whose sake, and in whose interest, then has he come?"

Mrs. Heatherley nurtures a hope, and Ethel strives to banish a thought, that both tend to the same point.

"He is more struck with my child than I could have believed a man would be, accustomed to the society of the most loveliest

women in London," Mrs. Heatherley thinks,
exultantly, and at the same time Ethel, struck
by the expression of her mother's face, is
telling herself—

" Mother is putting the father in the place
she wanted the son to fill the other day! I
hope he won't make an old goose of himself
and meet her views, and make my hard lot
harder than it is already. Oh, Walter! if
other men are ready to love me, *why* couldn't
you go on doing it? "

But while she is saying this to herself, she
is listening very attractively to the information Lord Monkstown is giving her about Boyne
Gate. He is telling her how it came into the
family generations ago, when a Baron Monkstown (this was before they were prompted
marquises) had fallen in love with a pretty
English girl, who turned out the heiress of
" Place," as the estate was called then, and
who returned her Irish lover's affection with
such romantic fervour, that she insisted on
changing the name of the estate of her
father's to Boyne Gate.

" This is the first time it has ever been let,"

he goes on to explain; "hitherto it has always been used as a dower-house; but, as I am unfortunate enough to have survived my wife, I have let St. Just have it for two or three shooting seasons."

"It's the only place you have in England, isn't it?" Ethel asks, for the sake of saying something. To her embarrassment, Lord Monkstown has succeeded in lagging behind the others, and courtesy has compelled her to stay and listen to his explanation; therefore she seems to be lagging, too.

"Yes; the only place I have in England, with the exception of a little house in Norfolk Street, that is scarcely worth speaking of, as it is only fit for bachelor's quarters."

"Mother has a house in Norfolk Street, too," Ethel says.

"Has she? Do you go to it for the season? Perhaps I shall be fortunate enough to have you for neighbours, if you go up for the winter gaiety! What is your number?"

Ethel tells him, and he exclaims—"Are you sure? that is very strange, for it's *my* number!"

"Yes, I am *quite* sure. We haven't been up for three years, but I can't be stupid enough to have forgotten the number."

"I bought it three years ago," he says, quietly; "perhaps your mamma may have sold it to me."

"Oh, no! I'm sure she hasn't, because she was speaking of her London house property the other day to the Bishop," Ethel says, with an air of conviction. Still, the subject seems to dwell in her mind with undue weight; for, when they are all settled into place around the luncheon-cloth, she says to Mrs. Heatherley, who is opposite—

"Mother, isn't it odd? Lord Monkstown has a house in Norfolk Street, and its number is the same as ours?"

In a moment each pair of eyes present are bent questioningly on Mrs. Heatherley, into whose pretty, fair face, a deeper tint comes for a moment, but there is not a touch of confusion in the way in which she answers promptly:

"It *would* 'be odd,' dear, if our house had not a distinguishing letter added to the num-

ber." Then with the easiest grace she turns
the conversation into another channel, along
which, with ready courtesy, Lord Monkstown
aids her to glide, and helpfully accompanies
her. But all the while he is thinking—
" That woman has parted with her property,
and has her own reasons for keeping quiet
about it."

The same thought enters into Miss Templeton's mind, and the Bishop groans in spirit as
he gives a furtive glance at her, and sees the
expression of malignant meekness which is
lighting up her face. " I shall hear of this
most unfortunate coincidence from Fanny,"
he says to himself, and mentally he resolves
to " keep Grove close to him all the day."

But his precaution, though he fully carries
it out, is of no avail. For the remainder of
the day he is protected from the assault of
daughterly-devotion, by his chaplain and the
home circle generally; but as soon as he is
left alone on his defenceless pillow at night,
his loved, but dreaded Fanny, takes him
unawares, and reduces him to a state of
abject misery :

" Papa," she whispers, creeping in with a little lamp in her hand, and her dressing-gown on, " I waited till I heard Perkins go away to the servants' wing, and then, as I couldn't sleep, I crept down. Did you hear that at luncheon ? "

" Did I hear what ? " he says, in a spirit of feeble prevarication.

" Why, about the house in Norfolk Street ? Don't you think that if it had been hers still, she would have said more than she did about the coincidence of the numbers being the same ? Of course she would ! Isn't she just the person to have twisted it into a link between herself and that old Marquis ! Oh ! papa, don't be weak ; do inquire into the state of her affairs ! In justice to me, don't hamper yourself with Mrs. Heatherley and her daughter, till you find that they can pay their own way."

The Bishop is frightened, undoubtedly frightened, by this fierce appeal to his paternal sense of justice, and his commonsense and honourable spirit of detestation of monetary entanglements. At the same time, frightened as he is about her, he is resolved to be very loyal to the best-looking, and most fascinating woman who has ever taken the trouble to show herself at her best before, and exercise her fascination to the utmost upon him.

"A pledge to marry is a very solemn thing, and the consideration of mere dross must not be permitted to interfere with its fufilment," he says, with as reverential, and at the same time august an air as he can manage, prostrate beneath the bed-clothes, with something suspiciously like a night-cap on.

But Fanny is inexorable. The attempt at being reverential and august does not strike awe into her heart for a moment:

"Nonsense, papa," she says, with emphasis, "it may be 'mere dross,' but you know how it upsets you to be short of it."

CHAPTER XI.

A PLOT.

ALTER GIFFORD has not confided the contents or nature of that fatal little note of Ethel's . to a single human being. It is always in his pocket and his thoughts; but he speaks of it to no one.

Nevertheless his sister knows as well as he does himself, that her shot has told, and that he has received his dismissal from Ethel Heatherley. And still, though she knows this, she is not happy!

Honestly and truly the disingenuous and cruel course she has taken, has been taken solely in what she mistakenly believes to be her brother's best interests. Therefore, it is disappointing and disheartening to her to see him glooming so terribly, now that she has won freedom for him, instead of making the highest use of that freedom, and seeking the love which Lily Somerset is willing to give him.

To do Lily Somerset justice, there has never been a moment during which she has displayed unmaidenly zeal to win him, since that interview between them which has been already recorded. On the contrary, she has rather stood aloof from him, being very kind and cordial when they are together, but never taking the turnings in the direction in which he *may* come, and never asking him when " he will come again," as the manner is of women, when the yearning for the society of the beloved object has overcome all reticence.

"Now this, in Miss Gifford's simple and unsuspicious eyes, looks too much indifference for her to let it pass uncommented upon long. Just as everything else seems to be *en train* for success, it is a little too trying to worthy Mabel that Lily should suddenly become careless and disencouraging.

" It seems to me that Walter may go or come, or stay away, so far as you're con-

cerned," she says, plucking up heart of
grace to speak her mind for the cause that
is so dear to her, even at the risk of
offending her resplendent young tyrant.

"He certainly may go and come as he
likes, without let or hindrance from me,"
Lily laughs.

"You don't tell me that you're tired of—
of *thinking* of him?" Mabel asks, aghast.

"Well, not that, certainly; but I am tired
of plodding on in my way, and of seeing him
plod on in his. I want to see some startling
change come to one of us. If I got suddenly
poor, and he got suddenly rich, your brother
would be so charged with pity and old asso-
ciations about unworthy me, that—I don't
know what might not happen; now, I am not
likely to get suddenly poor, but I am con-
sidering in my own mind how it would be
possible to put him in such a position, as
would compel him to put forth all his powers;
at present his practice is not engrossing
enough, or important enough. He moves
by inches; he thinks he is working hard,
whereas he is nearly exhausting his energies

in rolling a heavy ball filled with littleness up a steep hill."

As well as she can, Mabel follows the drift of these remarks, and as clearly as she can, extracts the meaning from them. Still, being human, she is liable to error, and she errs now in the deduction she draws.

"You mean that poor Walter ought to work harder, and make more money than he does"—she is beginning, when Lily interrupts her, sharply—

"I mean nothing of the kind. I mean that working chiefly as he does among a class who are not deemed of sufficient importance by their generous-minded fellow-creatures to have their well or ill-doing chronicled, and published, and wondered about—is like burrowing in the earth. I want him to come out into open places, and exercise his noble art upon those who are able to make him celebrated! I would not wish him to be anything more than he is —a good man, working well by stealth. But, for his own sake, for the sake of the restoration to health of his broken, weakened ambition, I would wish to see him a great man, Mab, and, if I tell you how he can become one, will you keep the secret?"

Of course Mabel promises, but she does it with a misgiving heart. It may be in irresistible Lily's mind to carry Walter off to. the altar, and marry him by force, the alarmed sister fears, and, if so!—how about the penalties which will befall those who are accessory to the deed?

Still the force of habit is upon her, and she promises!—hoping for the best.

Then for the first time in their intercourse, she sees Lily timid, and uncertain of herself.

" My plan is this—if you think it wise—"

Mabel starts so violently at this unwonted recognition of, and appeal to her wisdom, that Lily pauses to say, with a brief relapse into imperiousness—" Don't jump, and be absurd. If you think it wise, an opportunity offers itself, which, if taken, will put your brother in such a position that he will be *compelled* to be famous, and forced to blot out all the undermining memories and disappointments he nourishes and broods upon now. If you think it wise—that is, if you'll only say you're glad about it—I don't want any opinion from you, you know, Mab—Walter will have Dr. Laughton's practice, and with it he will take the onus upon himself of maintaining Dr. Laughton's magnificent reputation, and of justifying Dr. Laughton's acceptance of him as a successor."

"But, Lily, what can make Dr. Laughton give it up to Walter?" Mabel gasps, for Dr. Laughton is a prince among practitioners, the nodding of whose head, and the uplifting of whose eyebrows, puts fifty guineas in his own purse.

"Money, you goose, money!" Lily says, with a great assumption of superior worldly-wisdom, "and that's just the part of it that you are to keep *quite* secret; the money has been found, and the matter has been arranged; and now all that remains to be done is for Dr. Laughton to introduce Walter to his most important patients."

"Walter will never agree to it," Mabel cries, startled out of her customary awe of, and implicit, unquestioning obedience to aught that Lily decrees. " Walter will feel that he hasn't worked his way to it, and that it's your money has bought it, and, feeling that!—no Lily! I couldn't wish my brother to have so little spirit as to take it, grand as it would be."

Lily tries to fly into a passion, and fails in doing so for once in her life. In place of passion, scalding tears, the offspring of baffled, really good feeling, run down unbecomingly.

" How can you tell, how can you be so silly as to think, or to say that it is my money that has done it? How do you know that Walter hasn't other friends as willing to spend money upon him as I am, or, rather, as I would be if he needed it? Besides, how do you know that there's any money passed in the business at all? Dr. Laughton thinks an *enormous* deal of Walter's abilities; how can you say that, as Dr. Laughton is an old man, he hasn't been glad to give the good-will, or whatever they call it, to a worthy young successor?"

"I should like to think it," Mabel medi-
tates aloud; then she reminds herself ·and
Lily that—

" *You* told me it was 'money' made
Dr. Laughton give it up yourself, Lily,
and oh! what *shall* I do when Walter taxes
me with having deceived him, and reproaches
me with not having thought of his dignity
a little more. He will think it shocking,
and quite a thing that it would be impossible for a man of honour to do, to take
money for his own advantage from a
woman; it would be different if you were
old and ugly, my dear, indeed, it would!
But, I could never look my brother in the
face again, if I pretended to think he
would take such a great benefit from you."

"I can't be old and ugly all at once, can
I?" Lily says, trying to speak in a petulant
way, that she has frequently found efficacious
in bringing Mabel into prompt acquiescence
with her view of things. But to-day the
petulance fails her! The "reality" of
something higher and better than gratified
ambition or rewarded love, is forced upon

her. Faint and uncertain as these outlines, drawn by his faltering, frightened sister's hand, are, Lily sees something of the grand " unhasting, unresting " ´nature which she has been selfishly seeking to shackle with her little chains of gold.

"I can't be old and ugly all at once," she repeats, sorrowfully; "but it will *wither* me if what I have done lowers him in his own eyes—it can't in the eyes of anyone else." Then, with a quick change to indignation, at being misunderstood and trapped into making disclosures, she adds:

"And, how can you dare to say that it has been done in a way that could hurt the feelings of the proudest and most sensitively honourable man in the world?—and, even admitting that it has been done, who can say—who can tell him—that *I* did it?"

"Oh, Lily! your conscience accuses you, and your face betrays you," Mabel says, pushing her victory over filthy lucre to the utmost; "it would have been too terrible if my brother had fallen into such a trap for want of a word in season from me."

The supreme moment is over! and Lily is disgusted at the aspect of the generous action she has contemplated performing, when held up in this cold, rather coarse light.

"Don't waste any more seasonable words on me, Mabel; I know you're half right, and I am more than half wrong; still! what I've done, or wanted to do, won't be altogether so bad as to make me take the whole of the consequences to myself; get Dr. Laughton to be off his bargain—if you can; but, if ever you wish to speak to me after to-day, don't breathe a word of this to your brother —or, to me after now, when I close the subject, and fan it away!"

The way in which Lily wafts a huge, black, Spanish fan backwards and forwards, in a royally-fatigued, lanquishing way, as she says this, brings Mabel back into subjection, promptly.

"That you should be upset about either Walter or me—not but that Walter's worth a dozen of any other man *I* ever met with—"

"You've not met many"—this from the fairy tyrant.

" No, perhaps not, and the fewer the better
for me and all other women, I say ; but that's
neither here nor there, and what I want to
say shortly is—if you think of Walter rightly
you'll think that he is too high already in
the *right way* for either of us to help him
with mere money and good introductions ; a
peer's case will never be more to him than a
pauper's, my dear !—and, I do think, when
Dr. Laughton sees how really honest and
straightforward Walter is, that Dr. Laughton
will think twice."

" I'll never take the curb off good
intentions again, without seeing what the
road is before me," Lily says to herself,
remorsefully. Then she looks at Mabel, and
half-laughingly quotes—" A Daniel come to
judgment ! Oh, wise young man ! Oh,
good young judge !"

" I'm not a Daniel, neither am I wise or
good, but I know what's what, my dear,"
says Mabel, triumphantly, seeing she has
made an impression, and then Lily gets it
heavily for a few moments presently, in the
way of meek, soul-subduing, friendly casti-

gation, in a manner that is not to be contemplated in the ordinary manner of things.

And Lily has to admit that "What's what"
in this delicate minor key, is a knowledge
that is withholden from her. So she has
to possess her soul in unwonted patience,
and wait for the outcome of the best reso-
lution she has ever formed.

Will Walter take it? Will the man who
has given himself ungrudgingly to the most
irksome and unremunerative side of his professional labours yield suddenly, and consent
to be well-placed without sufficient labour
on his own part? Will he honourably—but
tamely—take a place he has not won? Will
he let a woman's hand carve his fortunes for
him while his own is strong?

These questions can only be answered by
Walter Gifford himself. And Walter Gifford
does not have an opportunity of answering
them until he is tongue-tied by considera-
tions which are forced upon him by other
people.

For example, Dr. Laughton calls on him,
and tells him in suave, courtly phrase, that

he does not desire to see himself succeeded by an abler man than Walter Gifford. Nor does the great practitioner, whose fiat has been fate in this neighbourhood for years, give his decision with a sordid motive. It matters little to him whether Walter Gifford succeeds him or not. He retires!—that is all! His retirement is the event, and no one knows better than himself that his successor must rely upon himself solely, just as much as though the "good-will" of Dr. Laughton had never been bought and paid for. But Dr. Laughton is a mere man, and is afflicted with a desire to stand well with pretty women; and Miss Somerset is the prettiest and most charming woman whom it has ever been in his power to serve! If selling his practice—which he wants to get rid of—will please her! well, he will sell it, and butter up young Gifford into the bargain, for young Gifford has it in him to make a bigger name than himself. It is in vain that Walter Gifford asks straightforward questions. Dr. Laughton evades them with the easy grace for which he is so justly celebrated. and

without uttering a word that can accurately
be called "untrue," he succeeds in giving
Mr. Gifford the impression that he has been
selected on his own merits to be the successor of the mighty medicine-man.

"From the day you came into the town I
have watched your career with the greatest
interest, and I give my unqualified approval
to the course pursued in every case that
has come under my notice," the courteous
physician says; and when Walter remarks
that, to the best of his knowledge, not one
of his cases has come under the great man's
notice, he is made to feel that he has raised a
petty quibble, and that there is something
puerile in going thus into details.

"You young men are very properly so
entirely absorbed in your own work, that
you have no perception of the cognizance
that is being taken of that work by older,
more experienced, and consequently less
absorbed men," Dr. Laughton explains,
quellingly.

"Still, I cannot comprehend the motive
which makes you select me, a stranger, when

there must be so many men equally deserving as myself, who have worked with you, and been taught by you," Walter urges.

" Put it down to an old man's caprice, if you refuse to think it a matter of sound judgment," Dr. Laughton says, for he is resolved to be loyal to pretty Miss Somerset, and to keep her secret to the end.

So the honour of succeeding Dr. Laughton on his own merits is thrust upon Walter almost against his will, and with reluctance he consents to the next move, which it is absolutely essential he should make, namely to go round under Dr. Laughton's wing, and be introduced to the more august patients.

He has few friends in Allerton Towers, none of whom he can take counsel now Ethel has cast him off, and he does shrink from taking this final step, which will seal the bond irrevocably, before he has expressed his doubts, and perhaps had them dispelled.

It will be more than useless to consult Mabel, he feels. That affectionate sister, and anything but profound woman, will see nothing out of the way in the transaction, but will probably regard it as merely a just and natural tribute to the extraordinary merits of her brother! Still, though he feels that she will be valueless as a counsellor, he must go to her for sympathy in this dilemma in which he finds himself placed. And, by going to her for sympathy, he knows that he will get it from some one else from whom he can scarcely ask for it direct.

Mabel is alone, rather to his disappointment, when he goes into the old-fashioned room at the Uplands, which is gradually getting the impress of Lily Somerset upon it. Out of the simplest materials Lily has brought grace and beauty.

A long, fish hamper seems an unpromising subject to deal with in the decorative way, at the first blush, but, treated by Lily, it seems as if no more fitting receptacle for ferns and heaths could be found. He recognises her hand, too, in the way in which a common, round, deal table has had its top covered with a cloth of velvety green moss, upon which wild flowers are studded artistically. The sight of these things bring the thought of her so vividly before him, that he exclaims at once, before even he gives his sister the customary salutation—

"Where's Lily?"

"Oh! Walter, she ran up to her room the moment she saw you coming;—don't be angry with her, my dear, she did it thoughtlessly, but she did it for the best," the poor lady blunders out, her mind so charged with the one subject, that she does not even notice her brother's look of supreme bewilderment.

"Angry with her!—did it for the best! —what in the world are you talking about, Mab?" he asks.

"Don't you know it yet?" she questions in return.

"Know what!—pray don't be enigmatical, Mab."

"Why, know about Dr. Laughton's practice?"

"I know that he has offered it to me— what has that to do with Lily?" Then he pauses suddenly, as the whole truth flashes upon him, and though his brow burns, and his blood gallops through his veins, there is no anger in his heart against Lily.

CHAPTER XII.

RESENTLY, after a pause, the solemn stillness of which frightens Miss Gifford into the vivid remembrances of the sacred promise as to secresy, which she has just—well! *nearly* broken, Walter says:

"Let me see Lily; she can't be silly enough to think that I can be annoyed with *her!*"

"You'll take it, then? Oh! Walter, my dear boy, I am so glad, though I never thought for a moment that you'd condescend so far as to take such a handsome offer, I mean favour, from any young lady—least of all from Lily Somerset, because of what has been, you know, and what you seem to have made up your mind never shall be again; and so I told her when she consulted me—I mean when she told me what she had done, and desired me to hold my tongue about it; 'No, Lily,' I said, quite firmly, 'hard as it is to gainsay any of your wishes, my duty to my brother compels me to tell you that this can *not* be;' and now I am so delighted to find that I was wrong, and that you are going to make Lily happy by letting her make you prosperous."

"My dear Mabel, you always think kindly on every subject, and wish for everybody's happiness," he says, gently, and his sister is nearly melted to tears by this recognition of her amiability, which, she instinctively feels, is a little tedious in its mode of expression at times.

"And now, will you let me see Lily? Ask her to come and speak to me," he says, taking advantage of the arrested flow of sisterly eloquence.

For the first time in her life, Lily Somerset's heart is beating rapidly from sheer nervousness. For the first time in her life, the spoilt child of fortune doubts the wisdom of one of her own acts, and fears what the consequences of it may be.

"If he would only have accepted the position without enquiry, and became famous and rich, I could have borne that he should never speak to me, or think of me again," the girl says to herself, as she stands clasping her trembling hands, longing, yet dreading, to be summoned to hear his fiat.

She has to lean against the dressing-table in order to support herself, when Mabel comes in, and she can hardly constrain her trembling to say—

"Well, Mabel! do you bring me the verdict? Does your brother think me an impertinent fool, for I see in your face you have told him."

"No, my dear Lily, that he does not, and *that* I did not; that is, you can't call it my telling him, when he jumped at it himself, in a way that looked like divination; and you would have been the last in the world, I'm sure, to wish me to perjure myself, and say I knew nothing about it, when all the time I knew everything; and he wants to speak to you, and he's so grateful and touched, that I believe things will end in a different way to what I feared; and—why, Lily!—what's this?"

"Only—only—" Lily tries vainly to stutter out an explanation, through the convulsively-repressed sobs, and the hot, rushing tears.

"I am not like myself," she goes on, struggling gallantly to regain composure. "I have made myself nervous staying up here alone, picturing Mr. Gifford's contempt for my impotent attempt to mould his career; and it has given me such a revulsion to hear that he is going to be friendly and kind."

Her words sound strangely in her own ears. Can she be the same spoilt, capricious, imperious Lily, whose own selfish will and pleasure have been of paramount importance to herself all her previous life. Can it be possible that the mere thought of having wounded or offended him can be causing her this exquisitely painful anxiety? She feels that her limbs tremble under her, and that her lips are quivering, as she goes down the stairs and into the room where he is waiting to judge and condemn her.

And something in the pleading, pale face, that is bent so wistfully towards him, makes him spring to meet her, in a sudden access of such pitying regard that she may be forgiven for mistaking it for love.

" Lily, your beautiful generosity, exercised so delicately, too, as it has been, touches me more than I can say," he says, warmly taking her hand ; and she draws her perfectly-balanced figure up proudly and happily, and her forget-me-not eyes beam gratitude and love upon him.

" You forgive me for daring to do something for you, and accept the poor service I can render, Walter ? " she asked.

He shakes his head, and all her unselfish hopes and aspirations for him fall down dead.

" I am more than strongly tempted to go into the groove, merely because you wish it and would put me there," he says, kindly ; " but look here, Lily, you'd be sorry yourself when you thought of it coolly, if I deserted the post I have gained for myself, and the people to whom I am useful. A man fills the niche into which he has fitted for himself, better than he can ever fill one into which he is pressed. The work I do in my own sphere is the work that has come in my way to do; it is ready to my hand; perhaps—who can tell—it might get neglected, or even not done at all—if I went away from it—"

"There is sickness, and suffering, and need of medical skill in the upper classes as well as in the middle and lower," she says, briefly, triumphing in the thought that she is using an unassailable argument.

"There is, Lily, and no man would more gladly strive to relieve that sickness and suffering than I would, if it came in my way in the course of things, and if I hadn't to neglect my plain and obvious duty in order to do it; but to gain, by purchase, a fresh field of labour, when the one that has been given to me needs all my care and skill, would be to leave undone my God-given work for my own worldly gain. Your own good heart will feel the truth of this, and teach you to pardon what, at first sight, looks like a churlish rejection of a sweet, gracious piece of womanly-kindness."

"And I was fool enough to fancy I could raise a man like you," Lily says, with such heart-felt admiration for what is best in him, in her tone, and look, that Walter admits to himself that his heart would go back to Lily, if Ethel Heatherley had never existed for him ;—"forgive my presumption, and—ask Dr. Laughton to find another successor."

" Do you mean ? "—Walter is beginning, when she interrupts him hastily—

" Yes, yes, I mean that exactly ; let the arrangement stand, don't *hurt* me by having anything returned ; you must know some clever doctor, and good man, who has a large family and no practice ; turn my feeble efforts to good account, Walter ; give me the joy of feeling that it has resulted in the welfare of some one better, and nobler, and more deserving than myself—will you ? "

" That I will, right heartily," he cries, and Lily tells herself, humbly, that she is scarcely worthy to be associated with this loyal, un-selfish nature, even in good works.

That Miss Gifford's disappointment, when she comes to hear the real state of the case, is not bitter, it is impossible to deny. For a few wild moments she has permitted herself to nurse the delusive hope that her brother would acquiescently slide into the position of local medical potentate, and be the wealthy and important person she always yearned to see him become, at the cost of the sacrifice of some of the loftiest conscientious scruples entirely! But still! "if Walter could do it, it would be right!" as she tells herself. And, now, to hear that all this anticipated honour and glory, and gold galore, is to be placed at the disposal of some unknown person, of unacknowledged worth and poor fortunes—

"It is trying, my dear, very trying," Miss Gifford says, mournfully, to Lily, and Lily's face beams brightly, as she answers, cheerfully—

"It is right."

A few days after this the Bishop returns to the Palace and Mrs. Heatherley to the cottage. The wedding day is fixed for an early date, and an extraordinary report gains credence in the neighbourhood, to the effect that

" a marriage is arranged between the Marquis of Monkstown and Miss Heatherley."

"My poor Ethel," Walter Gifford says to himself, when he hears this, " *my* Ethel, still, I know. Whose influence is it? No man but myself has any over her—it must be her mother!"

CHAPTER XIII.

AT LAMINGTON HALL.

LAMINGTON Hall, the seat of Sir John Hawtrey, Baronet, is one of the show places of the county. Local guidebooks go into ecstacies of enthusiasm over it; and after avowing that language cannot adequately describe its charms, generally wind up by declaring that it "almost rivals far-famed Chatsworth."

This, however, may be ascribed to local partiality, since those who know both places will fail to discern the faintest resemblance between them. Nevertheless, Lamington Hall is a very spacious and a very fine mansion, well anointed with that golden ointment which puts all things in the fairest light, and preserves all things in the most perfect order.

Its terraces are exquisitely arranged; mosaics, formed of flowers and foliage,

master-pieces of carpet-gardening all the
season through. Æstheticism finds no congenial corner at Lamington. Nothing tall
and ungainly in the way of sun-flowers or
white lilies, or hollyhocks are permitted to
mar the effect of the flat, low growth of
symmetrically-arranged beds. Somewhere,
away at the rear of the house, sheltering
the wing of the palatial stables, there is a
well kept "wilderness," in which nothing
is allowed to run wild, and where every
leaf seems to know and keep its proper
place.

The interior arrangements are quite as
admirably devised, and as effectually carried
out as the outdoor ones. Old Willesdon's
money is put to a good purpose, in so far
as keeping "Heaven's first law"—"Order"
—goes. Smoothly and noiselessly works all
the machinery of domestic management,
guided by the firm, strong hand, and the
great, good sense of the mistress of the
house, the baronet's only child, Caroline.

There is no doubt about Miss Hawtrey's
being a very wise dispensation. The great

heiress, who has fifty thousand a year in her
own right by her grandfather's will, is un-
swerving in the vigour and the zeal with
which she seeks out lurking extravagancies
and puts them down. There are moments
when the housekeeper and the butler loathe
their master's daughter, for she is not above
chronicling the flow of the very smallest beer.
And even the hens at the home-farm seem to
have an uneasy sense of duty undone on their
parts in the matter of egg-laying, when her
penetrating, cool eyes look them over as she
passes through, on the occasions of her
weekly visit of inspection.

This excellent gift of cautious prudence, in
every case in which money is concerned, is
not an inheritance from her lowborn mother,
the daughter of the Manchester Crœsus, but
is handed down to her in unimpaired integrity
by her well-descended, ostentatious, money-
loving, money-grudging father ; who contends
that he has not an atom of penuriousness in
his disposition because he cannot remember
the day on which he denied himself aught
which might tend to his own individual

comfort, or to the glorification of himself in the eyes of others.

And Caroline resembles him in most respects, but not in the matter of ostentation. She has not an atom of love of display in her nature. She cannot alter the order of things at Lamington because she is overruled by her father, who will have it said that his vineries and conservatories are the finest, and his carriages and horses the best-appointed in the county. But it pleases her better to drive about in a little unpretentious pony-carriage, than to sit in state in the huge family coach, or lounge in the elegant landau.

Then again in the matter of dress her tastes are plain almost to ugliness, her cousin, Lord Kenmare, thinks, when day after day he sees her come down to breakfast in a dull-hued, dowdily-made, gray dress, that gives her an air of quakerish simplicity. She has not a girl's natural love for flowers or jewellery, and never brightens herself up with a deftly-placed rose, or gathers lace about her throat gracefully, with a gold brooch. Magnificent diamonds and other gems repose in her

massive jewel boxes, but Caroline can rarely
be induced to deck herself in any of them.

"They suit me no better than a peacock's
tail would a little Jenny Wren," she says,
when her father signifies his desire that she
should array herself sumptuously, and shine
forth in the borrowed light of gems; "beautiful dress and brilliant jewels ought only to
be worn by beautiful and brilliant women—
they make me look smaller and more in-
significant than I am naturally."

Her humble opinion of her own personal
appearance is quite a genuine thing. In her
early childhood, when she was supposed to
be sleeping, an injudicious nurse remarked to
a nursery visitor that "Miss Caroline was an
ugly little thing sure enough, but that
wouldn't matter!—there would be plenty to
see beauty in her money." The remark sunk
into the childish heart, wounding it deeply at
the time, and leaving an impression that has
never been erased. Her money is the only
thing that man or woman finds attractive
about her, she believes. And so she goes on
her way, a self-contained, undemonstrative,

quiet little creature, whose one object in life
is to exercise a wise control over the riches
which have fallen to her share.

As may be imagined, there is little in common between this quiet, prudent, thoughtful
little lady, and her bright, rather reckless,
Irish cousin. He finds her dull and uninteresting, especially now that he knows
Ethel Heatherley, and she regards him as
one of the stars above her. But neither by
word, look, or sign will she let him discover
the secret of her heart.

Neither her father, nor her uncle, Lord
Monkstown, have said a word to her of
their wishes about Kenmare and herself.
But she has divined their wishes, and the
reason why Kenmare is made to stay at
Lamington, and the old, sore feeling comes
back to her heart as she sees that not even
the money which the old nurse prophesied
would make her beautiful, can win his
careless eyes to rest upon her for a moment,
approvingly. " He thinks me a dull, plain
little thing, and he's too honest to pretend
to think anything else, and I like him for

his honesty," she tells herself. But though she approves of the honesty, her heart aches for the cause of its being so displayed, and she goes on her daily round of duty with a feeling of bitterness that not all her sense of justice and reasonableness can enable her to cast out.

Instinctively she arrives at the truth, when, after that shooting-luncheon at Boyne Gate, Lord Monkstown comes home, and makes Ethel Heatherley his theme. As the father expresses his admiration, her eyes are quick to see the flush on Kenmare's brow, and she discerns that the son is righteously indignant at the possibility of having his father for a rival.

"Poor Kenmare!" she thinks; "if she only had half my money, how happy you might be; how crossly things go in this world! Poor Kenmare!"

Little observant as Kenmare is of her, he cannot but admit that his cousin does not lay herself out to attract him, or seek in any way to forward their fathers' plan. And so, after a time, feeling that he is safe with her, he

gives her a little more of his time and attention, and is rewarded by finding out that
the dull, uninteresting, unattractive little girl
whom he has been barely regarding as com-
panionable, even though he is a guest in her
father's house, is well informed on many sub-
jects that have an interest for him, and can
talk about them sensibly.

One morning he stops her just as she is
about to step into her little pony-carriage,
and drive herself down to the home-farm to
receive the weekly amount of the dairy and
poultry-yard produce. The pleasure she feels
in the fact of his coming to her thus volun-
tarily, finds no expression in either face or
manner. Unconsciously she fears that any
exhibition of liking on her part may check his
friendly feeling, and drive him from her, and
she is beginning to dearly love the intercourse
with him, prosaic and void of sentiment as
it is.

"Where are you going?" he asks, coming
up to her swiftly, "I want you for a few
minutes, to tell you something that has
disgusted me awfully!"

"Can you wait till I come back from the farm?" she asks, indifferently, though her heart leaps with pleasure when he says—

"Why can't I go to the farm with you? Yes! let me come, and send your groom away; I can open the gates and hold the pony while you're pottering about down there."

"You can come if you please; and I shall not want you, William," she says, placidly, but if Kenmare had eyes for her, he would see a colour on her face and a light in her eyes that only the painter, Love, can put into a woman's face.

"You heard my father speak of those people who have been staying at Boyne Place?"

"Do you mean the Bishop and his daughter, or the widow who is going to marry the Bishop and *her* daughter?" she asks.

"I mean the widow, Mrs. Heatherley and —Ethel—that's her daughter's name. Ethel Heatherley is the only girl I've ever cared for, and I love her more than a fellow ever loved a girl before, I believe, and I've told her so, and she wouldn't have anything to say to me, because she was engaged to a man—a doctor at Allerton Towers. And, now, this morning, my father shows me a letter from her mother 'accepting the offer of his lordship's hand for her daughter!' Carry, it's monstrous, when I love her so; my own father, too! it's horrible."

"Did Lord Monkstown know of your— your love for her?"

"I never told him it was Ethel; but once, when the question of my marrying somebody else arose, I told him that I cared too much for a girl already ever to think of marrying another one; but it's not that, Carry. I'm not unreasonable enough to blame my father; he has a right to ask her to be his wife, knowing nothing of my affair; but how can she have brought herself to accept him?"

"How, indeed!" Caroline murmurs; then half-fearing that she may have partially betrayed herself by those two words, she goes on, collectedly—

"I understand it is her *mother* who has accepted him for her daughter; from the little

I have heard of Mrs. Heatherley I should
think she is a scheming, ambitious woman,
just the one to accept my uncle's offer, without her daughter's knowledge, and then work
on the girl to redeem her mother's promise;
don't condemn Miss Heatherley, till you know
more about it, Kenmare."

He looks at her more wistfully, and with
more interest than he has ever shown in her
before, and says:

"'Pon my word, you're a kind little thing,
Carry! I felt I must speak to someone about
it. When my father spoke to me just now,
and showed me Mrs. Heatherley's letter, I felt
stunned, and it was all I could do to keep
myself from bursting out with the truth; but
I reminded myself that it would be a frightful
thing, if this great calamity does come to
pass, for him to know that I had wanted her
myself; so I pulled myself together, and got
away as quickly as I could."

"I am very, very sorry," she says, earnestly.

"That's very good of you," he responds,
heartily; "someway or other, I didn't expect

much sympathy from you. I thought you'd regard anything of the nature of love as bosh and nonsense, and only think me a fool for being unable to get over my disappointment."

"Oh, no! I can quite understand a man loving a beautiful girl, like Miss Heatherley; beauty is a great gift! the most precious possession a woman can have, I think, for it wins the only thing worth winning in life—real love."

The girl speaks with an intensity and fervour that astonishes her companion, and covers herself with confusion, as soon as she ceases speaking.

"I shouldn't have thought you felt like that," he says, wonderingly. "You give me the idea of being so *very* full of commonsense, that I fancied you had never given a thought to the trivial matter of love in your life."

"Perhaps I haven't for myself; but I have thought a great deal about it for other people."

"But you're wrong about the beauty, you know; it isn't only beauty fellows care for; there is something else, and every woman,

who's anything at all, has that something else.
I believe, for some fellow, if he only happens
to meet her."

She shakes her head solemnly.

"Not every woman; I haven't it," she says.
and she is innocent of all wish to extract a
compliment from him.

"You don't know that," he says, en-
couragingly, but there is no strong air of
conviction about his manner of saying it.

"You don't know that! it's only that you
haven't met the man with the right, clear
sight to see it: I daresay you have had any
number of professed worshippers after you,
now haven't you? Girls with such fortunes
as yours always have."

She winces; and the same look of mortified
pain which swept over her little face when
she heard her nurse's words long ago, sweeps
over it now. But she forces herself to say
quite calmly:

"Yes, my money has had many worshippers; there are many men who would cumber
themselves even with me, for the sake of my
fortune."

It is a difficult speech to answer. The speaker's humble opinion of her own *personnel* is so evidently unfeigned, that he, half-sharing it as he does, does not think it worth his while to deprecate or combat it. Accordingly, he diverges abruptly from the subject of her lack of charms, and returns to the one that is absorbing all his thoughts.

"Though I can't have her myself, I should never have been utterly wretched if Ethel had stood to her guns, and married her doctor; but if *this* thing is true I shall go away, and I shan't very much care where I go, or what becomes of me; to think of her as my father's wife! To think of her selling herself in such a way will be maddening!"

"Hope still that it is merely her mother's consent which has been given; I don't believe the girl lives who could take your father after refusing you; it would be impossible, unnatural!"

She speaks so fervently that he cannot doubt any longer that she will prove a real true friend to him. A friend to whom he

may, with safety and assurance turn in any
time of trouble or distress. A good, sensible
girl, who will give him a sister's quiet love,
listen patiently to the story of any difficulties which may assail him, and, if needful,
give him advice and sympathy! All this
her tone seems to promise him, and it never
occurs to him, that such a sensible, plain girl
as she is, can be actuated by any warmer
feeling than this " friendship," on which he
is so confidently relying.

"It does me good to hear you speak in
that way, Caroline," he says, cheerily. His
sanguine spirit has revived under the influence
of her sympathetic words, and he almost
fancies that her instinct against the possibility
of Ethel committing the enormity of marrying his father, must be a correct one, " I wish
I could get you to know Ethel! You'd plead
my cause for me like a little brick, I know,"
he says, enthusiastically.

"No one can do that for you. This is the
dairy; shall we stop here or drive up to the
house?"

"Up to the house I think; anything to

prolong the pleasure of driving with you,
Carry," he says, so up to the house they
go, and Mrs. Hocking, the farmer's wife,
stabs Caroline right through the heart, by
whispering, meaningly—

"Pleased to see the gentleman, and more
than pleased, Miss Hawtrey! I've heard two
or three words, but didn't like to take any
notice, till I saw you driving up together,
so cosy and happy, just now; I s'pose it
won't be long before we lose you now, Miss?"

These words are half-whispered, but still
they are designed for the gentleman's ears as
well; and feeling sure that he hears every
one of them, Caroline is too proud to attempt
to arrest the torrent of Mrs. Hocking's eloquence.

"This gentleman, is only my cousin, Lord
Kenmare, Mrs. Hocking; you are quite mistaken in supposing that he will ever be
anything else to me," she says, with cold
dignity, and Kenmare thinks "she really
needn't be quite so serious about such an
utterly absurd mistake."

The rest of the visit to the farm is very

pleasant—to Kenmare. Now that he has broken the ice, and discoursed of his love to Caroline, his spirits have risen considerably, and he is quite happy and at ease. It amuses him to see her gravely going through the business of auditing the accounts which are submitted to her, and it interests him to see her eight perfectly-matched Jersey cows, and her various runs of rare poultry.

"Cut out for an old maid," he says to himself, as he marks the orderly way in which she has everything kept, and the thorough precision with which she contrives to have all her directions carried out. "Cut out for an old maid! but a dear, sensible little piece of ice for a friend for all that; how she would laugh at the governor's suggestion, that I should make up to her. Awful joke it would be to tell her."

END OF VOL. I.

www.ingramcontent.com/pod-product-compliance
Lightning Source LLC
Chambersburg PA
CBHW020104030726
47498CB00006B/1943